THE INNKEEPER'S WIFE

THE INNKEEPER'S WIFE

A FRIENDSHIP LIKE NO OTHER

JOAN T. BROUSSARD

To Father Don Piraro and Sister Lucy Silvio
who helped me to look within myself
deep enough to discover Gertrude in me.
And to Carl, my husband, who has welcomed
and loves Gertrude as much as I do.

ACKNOWLEDGMENTS

I would never have discovered Gertrude within if it had not been for the instruction I received from Father Don Piraro on Ignatian spirituality and imaginative contemplation method of prayer. I am grateful that he taught me this prayer way. It has become my favorite way to pray. This book gives witness to the fruit of such prayer. His training in my spiritual director program gave me the tools to enable integration of all Gertrude's gifts and talents. Thank you, Father Don. I love you.

Sister Lucy Silvio encouraged the use of imaginative contemplation that resulted in my discovery of Gertrude. As my spiritual director, she helped me to look deeper in myself to discover all God wanted to reveal. My Gertrude was looking to emerge; Sr. Lucy and I made her feel welcomed and loved.

I especially am grateful to a colleague, Nelda Turner, who shared her "Gertrude" with me. Thank you, "Strawberry." These two are quite a pair.

I wish to thank each of my directees who have allowed me to help them discover their Gertrude and begin their own discovery process.

I acknowledge my grandchildren who recognize when Gertrude is out to play.

I am extremely grateful to my lifelong friend, Virginia Gail Evans, who first glimpsed Gertrude many years ago and asked to be her friend. Thank you for being my friend, my sister.

I am so thankful to those who know me as Tootie, which is the first name Gertrude ever had.

INTRODUCTION

THE STORY YOU are about to read is fiction, but it could have really happened. Scripture tells us of the inn when Joseph and Mary went to Bethlehem for the census. It also speaks of the innkeeper who gave them the stable because there were no more rooms. It is conceivable that the innkeeper had a wife. Jewish custom dictated that men were not allowed at the birth of children. So it is very plausible that a woman would have been present to be midwife to Mary's delivery. Why couldn't it have been the innkeeper's wife?

I have chosen creative license over historical accuracy. This is intentional as I prefer to present the result of this powerful prayer of imaginative contemplation, which is not bound by context. Rather it is only concerned with the prayer and Gertrude's acceptance of God's presence and message communicated. This is evidenced, for example, by the fact that my main character, Gertrude, does some journaling of her prayers. Prayer journaling is a relatively modern concept, and most women of Jesus's time were not well educated, but Gertrude is special in so many ways that it only seems logical she has the ability to read and write. So while I ask you to come with me on this biblical voyage, let your mind open and come join Gertrude in an amazing journey.

St. Ignatius of Loyola taught a way of prayer using imaginative contemplation. This prayer method involves entering into the scripture scene as one of the people present, as an observer to the scene or as one's self who would participate in the event described in Scripture.

I have loved this method of praying ever since it was first introduced to me by Father Don Piraro, the director of the St. Charles Retreat Center in Lake Charles, Louisiana, when I was training to become a spiritual director. I have used this type of prayer to be present at the nativity, with the woman at the well, at the Last Supper, and, more profoundly, at the time of Jesus's passion.

This story of the innkeeper's wife is the result of imaginative contemplation. I was on an eight-day retreat at the birthplace of St. Ignatius in Azpeitia, Spain. It was in the spring, and my spiritual director, Sister Lucy Silvio, suggested I use the nativity for meditation during my retreat. I remained with this mediation for the duration of my eight-day retreat, writing down every conversation, every thought I had, and every prayer that came to mind. I wrote my own Magnificat as suggested by Sister Lucy. This story emerged from that prayer experience.

In my first prayer time, I began by picturing in my mind the inn as Joseph entered to ask for a room. As the innkeeper sent him to the only space available, I heard the voice of a woman scolding him. The woman had noticed the pregnant young woman on the donkey just outside the inn. I immediately recognized her voice as my own. This began my spiritual experience of helping to midwife Mary with the birth of her son and the beginning of a friendship with the woman, her husband, and her son.

The time I spiritually spent together with this family for these eight days will forever be at the core of my faith. She handed me her baby as soon as it was born. It was my choice whether or not to accept her son. Then to have him walk with me to meet the Father was the glorious culmination of my retreat. Advent holds a special significance in light of this retreat and the experience of the birth of Jesus and our growing relationship since. I know of no better way to describe this experience than to share the conversations I had with Mary, Jesus, and finally with the Father. I wrote about each in my journals. I humbly offer parts of my journaling for your prayerful reflection. They are included in the appendix.

I am so grateful that Our Lady did not let the painful ride deter her from the will of the Father. The message for us is "Don't get off the donkey!"

My retreat in Azpeitia, Spain, ended with the grace of a renewed faith and love for the Father. I pray that he will always be glad to see me approach. I approach often. In the words of St. Ignatius, "God will give to us the extent and depth and breadth that our soul is open to receive. So let our soul and spirit be open to *all* that God has for us. Let Him shower us with the gifts of His Spirit and all the gifts under the heavens."

The book you are holding has emerged from my retreat experience. There is a Gertrude in each of us. Your habits and sinful behavior may be different than those of Gertrude, but the struggle is the same. The good news is also the same. Jesus offers himself as ransom for our sin and paid the price. He is offering forgiveness and love to each of us. All that is required is that we open our heart and accept him. The result is a life of peace, of joy, and of so much love. Won't you consider following Gertrude's example—accept the baby, accept Jesus? And don't forget the message Mary has to offer—say yes and don't get off the donkey.

One last note to you, the reader. I offer this story as an invitation for you to "accept the baby" and allow Jess to speak to you of his love. I have taken *big* literary license in presenting Gertrude in the same spirit as when I pray *big*. Gertrude's story, though fictional, offers a lesson that transcends time. It was true for her, and it is true for us today.

1

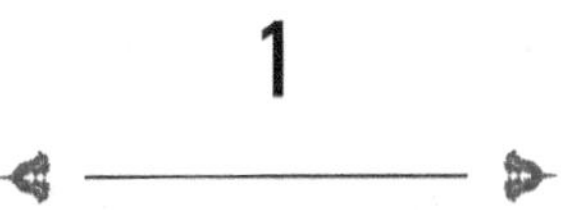

Rejoice always. Pray without ceasing.
In all circumstances give thanks,
for this is the will of God for you in Christ Jesus.

—1 Thessalonians 16–18 (NAB)

I HAD BEEN working in a frenzy for the past several months. As soon as the word of the census spread throughout the city, my husband, Eli, had the employees and me preparing. There was so much preparation to do: weaving to complete, linens to wash, food to gather, and so much to clean. We cleaned every room nearly every day, but it was amazing how much dirt still accumulated, even when you got down on your hands and knees to scrub the old, worn bricks.

On this day, we only had one room available. It was the smallest and darkest of the rooms we had to offer, which was why it was left to fill last of all. It was the room I was the most ashamed of, but there was nothing I could do about it. It offered very little light or warmth. My husband was just the manager of this inn; we weren't the owners, so we couldn't make any changes to the actual structure. The best I could do was to open the tiny window and let a slight breeze come in to air out the linens. I put a fresh vase of flowers on the tiny dresser and fluffed the straw mat.

"Gertrude," Eli called up the stairs. "Gertrude, please come down here."

I sighed quietly and smoothed the front of my dress down and tucked a stray hair back under my veil before I made my way downstairs. Eli knew my list of chores was never-ending, and yet he constantly insisted on calling me away from my work. And usually it only added to my list of things to do. But I bit back any sharp retort I might let slip.

"Yes, husband?" I asked when I arrived at the reception desk.

He ignored me at first as he looked over the ledger in front of him. I recognized our accounts ledger, one that I normally took care of. I was fortunate in the fact that I could write and do math quite well. It was not common for women to have this type of education. My father was a forward thinker and wanted me to be self-sufficient in case I was ever left on my own as was the case of many women we knew who were widowed. They were left at the mercy of men who treated them as little more than slaves. He wanted me to have the ability to read and write, which gave me a better chance of a good life. I often wrote my petitions to God on old discarded ledgers from the inn. The backs of those pages provided a lot of space to write my prayers to God, many of which were to ask him to help me curb my tongue and to consider the feelings of others. I am usually prone to speaking before thinking, a trait I try to control without much success. It was very typical for my words to come bubbling out—interrupting whomever was talking. This was something I have been aware of and worked hard to overcome.

As it turned out, my education was a benefit to Eli when we married and began to manage the inn. He was very good with maintenance and greeting people. I preferred to read, weave, and take care of the books. Many of the people who stayed at the inn were travelers on their way to other places and provided little companionship. I prayed often that God would send someone with a wife who would stay long enough for a friendship to begin. While I considered Eli my best friend, I hungered for another woman to share my thoughts and feelings with, woman-to-woman.

I waited quietly before he finally looked up at me. "I think we should make the stable ready for visitors," he said.

"Husband, are you mad? How insensitive of you. The stable? We couldn't possibly have anyone stay there, much less charge them to stay in that place."

He looked at me levelly. "People are flooding into the city, and we only have the one little room left. We can't miss out on this opportunity. I need you to make sure some of the stalls get cleaned out and prepare some bedding and linens to put out there just in case."

I opened my mouth to argue, but the look on Eli's face silenced me. Instead, I nodded and went outside to find one of the stable boys to begin mucking out the stalls. Unfortunately, the stable was rather full as well with the animals of our guests. Luckily, the weather was nice enough that many of the horses and other animals could be kept outside, which freed up the stalls. Our own animals, like the pigs and chickens, had their own pen area further away.

It took me a few minutes of searching before I found one of the stable boys asleep on the side of the barn. I shook him awake and told him to start cleaning. Then I went back inside the inn to finish working on my other tasks.

I went by the kitchen to see how lunch was coming along as noon was fast approaching. It was hot in the kitchen with the fire going, but the smell was amazing. The women who sometimes helped me the in kitchen when we were busy were great cooks. There were bowls of dried dates and figs and candied apricots. The evening meal would also include sweet meats, nuts, lentils, and dried fish. The warm bread sat covered by a cloth, and a thick, hearty stew was boiling in a large pot. It smelled delicious, but I would have to wait until all of our guests had their fill before I could begin on my own lunch.

I bustled back upstairs to the third floor of the building where Eli and I made our home. It was a cramped space, but with all of the windows thrown open, it felt bigger than it actually was. I liked the view as well. From one side of the building, I could see the hustle and bustle of Bethlehem, but from the other side, I could look at the peaceful farmlands. My favorite spot was the stone bench near the window. I spent many hours there, writing, praying, and wondering when Yahweh would finally send the Messiah he'd promised, as taught by our Jewish rabbi. I have always been an impatient woman, and being impatient with Yahweh was something he surely must be used to by now. Seeing so many people come through the inn and witnessing so much unkindness, greed, and lack of compassion of some made me very impatient for the promised Savior to come and hopefully provide a way for people to change. I needed a Savior and so did they.

Eli always begrudged being outside of the main city center, but I quite enjoyed it. It was more peaceful out here. Granted, it meant we didn't get the same foot traffic as those establishments further in, but we did enough business to always turn a profit. It was nice that we were able to live in the building as well. We didn't need much space and were content.

Though we had been married for nearly ten years, we still didn't have any children. I had been pregnant twice before, but both pregnancies ended in sorrow. The first baby boy lived only three days, while the second was stillborn. Each time, it felt as though a small part of me had been ripped away. I tried not to let it harden my heart, but there were times when I would sit in my window and watch the families around me. Then my heart would fill with jealousy. I was truly tested when our nearest neighbor had a little boy. He was now two years old, and he would run around in the grassy field. Sometimes his father would chase him, and they would collapse in fits of laughter. It made my stomach clench, knowing I could not provide that for Eli.

The only thing that got me through the day was to pray to God. I wrote down many of my prayers in a small book I kept under my prayer bench near the window. It helped me when things were difficult to reflect on that point in my life when I was at my lowest. But God was always there to help me and renew my faith. I knew the only thing that would keep me going was to stand faithful, pray big, and look for some blessing in my life somewhere. I knew that my children were with Yahweh, and that gave me some consolation. Although I knew that they were his first, I still felt a great pain of loss when I allowed myself to think of each delivery and the loss of the future they represented.

I was reflecting on my children up in heaven as I began to sort through some of our spare linens. As I dug through my old wooden chest, I found the swaddling blankets I had made for each child. These blankets were my finest work. I held the blanket up to my face. It was soft and smelled fresh and clean. I prayed to God in that moment that someday a baby would find comfort in that bit of linen. I loved weaving these blankets and was quite skilled at it. I added to our income by selling them to travelers staying at the inn. They marveled at the intricate patterns and fine quality of the fabric woven by my hand.

I laid the blankets and swaddling clothes carefully back in the chest and pulled out some other blankets to put out in the stable. I figured if any guests happened to be put out there, the least I could do for them was provide them with some comfortable blankets to sleep with. I shook each one out and darned any holes that moths had eaten in them. Then I folded each blanket up in neat little squares before taking them downstairs.

The lunch hour was over, and I could finally sit down for a moment and rest while I savored the remaining stew. The balance of meat and vegetables in that savory broth was enough to sustain me for the rest of the day. Eli joined me, but he didn't speak much. "You should rest for a few hours," I said. "You look so tired. You've been on your feet all day."

He rubbed his forehead. "There is just too much to do. The order I put in from our usual grocer hasn't come in, and I don't know if we'll have enough food for tomorrow. Jeremiah has promised to have the order brought over as soon as it arrives, but with all of the visitors in town, he's swamped as well and has to bring produce in from farms farther away."

I reached over and placed my hand on his and gave him a reassuring squeeze. "Tell me what the cooks need. I'll go out and see what I can find to tide us over. Maybe I can think of some substitutes if I can't find what they have asked for."

"Thank you, Gertrude. That would be a huge help." He gave me a smile and a peck on the cheek after he had listed off all of the items needed.

I was surprised at just how much we were in need of. There were a lot of spices but also many vegetables and flour. He mentioned sugar as well, but I knew that was one item we could easily cut if it wasn't available. We had a lot of fresh fruit from our own trees behind the inn and a bit of honey, and that could do in a pinch.

I grabbed my basket and tucked the money Eli had given me into a small money purse I kept tied to my belt and set off into the city. It was clear as soon as I stepped out the front door that there were many more people in the city than normal. The streets were crammed with people on foot and carts pulled by horses, oxen, and donkeys. The census created chaos in the streets that were not big enough to handle the influx of so much humanity. It was louder than normal with people yelling at each other, but I knew just where to go. I slipped in out of the throngs of people easily as I made my way to the street where most of the farmers came to sell their goods.

It was a much quicker trip than I had anticipated. It was much easier for me to purchase the goods we needed. I found good substitutes for the things that were not available. Of course, I talked with the farmers who knew my skill at bargaining, and before long, I was able to negotiate a good price for everything even though others were paying a higher price because everything was in higher demand. I am often impatient but always a shrewd businesswoman. As expected, though, I couldn't find any sugar. Our guests would just have to do without the desserts our cook had planned for the menu until some became available. My own sweet tooth would have to go on a fasting this day.

Satisfied that I had purchased most of what we needed with a little of our money left, I was in a good mood as I made my way back to the inn. There were so many new faces out in the streets, and all of the other inns were bursting at the seams with guests like we were. This census was a lot of work, but it meant many of Bethlehem's businesses would easily make a profit for the year, ensuring our survival.

The long walk back also gave me a moment to be with God. I was able to block out the noise as I got to the edge of the city and have a talk with him. "Lord," I said under my breath, "please, give Eli strength and wisdom. I know what a toll this census is taking on him. I'm doing what I can to make sure that he doesn't overwork himself, but I need a bit of your help. He works himself so hard, and I fear that his health may pay the price. I also pray that you guide his decisions. He means well, but his strong work ethic and the promise of a dollar can sway him. I look to you in all things. I am very grateful to have him as my husband and my friend. He has always taken good care of me. Thank you, Father. Amen." Then I said to myself, *I'll have to write that prayer down when I get a chance. It's one I want to pray more often.*

As soon as I walked in the door, I was greeted by my husband. He had a big smile on his face that I recognized as the one he wore for paying guests. When I looked into the small sitting room, I saw a man sitting by the fire in one of the rocking chairs.

"Gertrude, we have a new guest here. As soon as you drop the groceries in the kitchen, would you mind making sure his room is ready?"

"Of course, husband, are we putting him in the little room upstairs? It's our last," I asked in a quiet tone. I looked over at the man again. He was young and seemed to have an easy manner. He didn't seem at all bothered about having to wait a little while longer for his room to be ready.

"Where else would we put him?" my husband asked, still with that wide smile.

"Well," I said delicately, "he's a young man. Maybe he wouldn't mind staying in the stable so we can save the room in case another guest with a family comes along."

Eli's smile fell. "He paid more than that room is worth. Please, Gerty, go make it ready."

I nodded and set about to the task. I knew in Jewish marriages that the wife would never dare to contradict her husband, especially in public. My husband often took my advice to heart, but he ultimately made the final decisions concerning the running of the inn. I knew when it was my time to stop arguing, and this was one of them. He wasn't mean or harsh about it; we had an understanding between ourselves, which made our marriage comfortable. But it didn't mean I always had to like his choices; I just had to respect him enough to obey. And I did.

Dinner was ready after the new guest was settled in upstairs, and night was already starting to fall. I stepped out the back door for a moment to breathe in the fresh air while the guests ate in the large dining room. I wrapped a shawl around my shoulders against the gentle breeze that was turning cold. The sun had just dipped below the horizon, and I looked up at the stars. I loved sitting out in the evening after a long day to gaze at the sky and marvel at Yahweh's creation. I always felt little, and he felt so big.

The moon was still low in the sky, and the lights from the city seemed so far away. The stars however were unusually bright this night. One star in particular seemed to stand out more than the others. We had been hearing people talk about this star that was brighter than others and why it would appear about our little town. This pinprick in the sky seemed special, as though God was winking and making a promise to me that something great was on its way. I couldn't quite put my finger on it, to be honest. This night I had a strong feeling that my life was going to change. I had a sense of excitement, of anticipation—of what, I wasn't sure.

2

If You Want

If you want, the Virgin pregnant with will
come walking down the road,
pregnant with the holy, and say, "I need shelter for the night.
please take me inside your heart, my time is so close."
Then, under the roof of your soul, you will witness
the sublime intimacy, the divine, the Christ,
taking birth forever, as she grasps your hand for help,
for each of us is the midwife of God, each of us.
Yes there, under the dome of your being
does creation come into existence
externally, through your womb, dear pilgrim — the sacred
womb of your soul,
as God grasps our arms for help:
for each of us is his beloved servant, never far.
If you want, the Virgin will come walking down down the street,
pregnant with Light and sing.

—St. John of the Cross

The breeze picked up, and I shivered, pulling my shawl tighter to my shoulders before heading back inside to the warmth of our sitting room. I spent many evenings by the fire, darning clothes or weaving some new linen. Occasionally, I was joined by a couple of the guests who were looking for company. It was always a pleasure for me to hear about their travels and where they came from. I found it exciting to hear their stories.

This night, however, I was alone by the fire. Everyone had already gone up to bed, except Eli, of course. He kept late hours, checking the ledgers and double-checking our storage to ensure we had enough food until the next shipment came. It was a packed house, so I knew it meant extra work for him.

I was surprised at how quickly my eyes began to droop from exhaustion. When I had nearly nodded off, I decided it was time to put away my sewing and head to bed. It had been a long day, or week rather, and it wasn't over yet. There would still be a couple more busy weeks ahead for us before the crowds coming for the census would slow and we could take a break.

"I'm going upstairs now. Are you coming soon?" I asked.

"Yes, I'll be up in just a moment. I need to check some things before I come to bed," my husband replied.

I kissed him on the cheek as he bent over his books before I began my trek upstairs. But not halfway up, I heard the front door open. Naturally curious, I stopped in my tracks and listened in. I knew it wasn't polite to eavesdrop, but I was curious about who would be coming in so late in the day.

"Good evening, sir," my husband said. "How can I help you?"

"I am sorry to bother you so late, but I am looking for a room for my wife and me. She's pregnant, and every other inn we've gone to is full. My wife is tired, so any accommodation you can make for us would be a great help," the man replied, obviously weary from a long journey.

I heard my husband close his ledger, and I could tell he was going to try and broker a deal with this poor man. I slipped down the stairs and peeked out the door to see the young woman sitting on a donkey, obviously well advanced in her pregnancy.

"All of our rooms are full in here, but I have some space in the stable. It's not much, and I wouldn't charge you the same rate as a regular room, but we can make it comfortable enough."

The man hesitated, clearly torn between wanting to let his wife rest and an aversion to sleeping in a barn. "Okay, thank you so much. We will take the stable."

"I'll send my wife out shortly with some blankets to make the place comfortable."

The door closed, and I waited until my husband had poked his head around to shout up the staircase. "Oh, Gertrude," he said, surprised seeing me standing right behind him. "I'm glad you're still awake. I need you to take blankets and things out to the stable. We have two guests staying the night there."

Before he could barely finish his request, my anger got the best of me. "Eli, didn't you see the woman? She is pregnant. How could you send a pregnant woman to sleep in the barn?" I asked furiously. "She needs a proper bed to sleep on."

"All of the rooms are full," he replied. "They didn't have to accept my offer."

"I knew you should have saved that last room and made that other man sleep out there. You cannot charge that poor family to sleep with those animals."

"Gertrude, you don't understand business. This is how you make a profit, and it's all about supply and demand."

"I don't care about the money. I care about the people." I crossed my arms over my chest. "Well, if you are going to charge him for the room, I'm not going to charge them for food. They can eat for free as long as they stay here."

There were times when I knew to not argue with my husband, but there were also times when he knew not to argue with me, and this was one of them. He gave me a rueful smile and consented. It felt like a small victory, but I wasn't going to push my luck any further. Besides, I needed to get those blankets before it got too late so the couple could get settled in.

I rushed back to the front room where I had separated out those linens earlier in the day and found the best ones. They were soft and beautiful. We didn't get many women through the inn, mostly tax collectors, textile merchants, and other peddlers. It was the rare treat for a family to be traveling through and stopping for a night's rest. I knew it could sometimes be a bit daunting for women to be around such rough men who didn't always exhibit the best manners. I always tried to make the women as comfortable as possible. And maybe this time, God would answer my prayer for a friend.

I looked out the window toward the stable and saw the man helping his wife down from their donkey. Oh, she looked so very pregnant as though that baby were to come any minute. Just at that moment, the woman bent forward and grasped her husband's arm with one hand while the other went straight to her protruding belly. I heard a faint cry drift across the yard.

"Oh dear," I said to no one. "That baby is on its way into the world."

I quickly dug into the chest once more and found the little swaddling blankets. "Lord, you heard my prayer earlier. A baby will be warmed by these after all."

I gathered up the linens and headed straight to the barn. There was no time to waste.

3

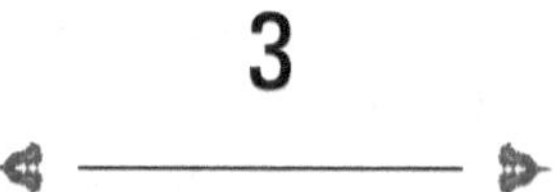

While they were there,
the time came for her to have her child
and she gave birth to her first born son.
She wrapped him in swaddling clothes
And laid him in a manger,
because there was no room for them in the inn.

—Luke 2:6–7 (NAB)

I DIDN'T BOTHER to knock as I let myself into the barn. I was happy to see that the stable boy had done a decent job at cleaning out two of the stalls. I would have been embarrassed otherwise. The smell was just something they would have to get used to. There was no getting rid of it while the animals still shared the nearby space. But there was plenty of fresh hay to make the space warm and comfortable.

"Excuse me, I don't mean to barge in here," I said as I peeked around one of the low walls.

The man was standing next to his wife who was leaning over one of the troughs. She had her hands on the edge of the basin and took deep breaths as her husband rubbed her back. It was truly a beautiful sight.

"Oh," the man looked up at me. "No, it's all right. It's just that my wife has gone into labor. She has been having birth pains for the last three miles. I could tell even though she never said anything to me."

As if to punctuate the statement, a small moan escaped the woman's mouth.

"Just breathe, my lady, and I will prepare a spot for you to lean back on," I said as I started to move the straw around and lay out the blankets. "I'm so sorry my stubborn husband sent you here to this dingy old stable. You can believe I scolded him good. I told him just today that we should saved the last room in the main house for any special guests who might come along with a special need, but he insisted on making a profit. There, that should do fine."

I turned to her to help escort her over to the newly made bed, but as soon as I offered out my arm, the woman stopped still. A gush of water splashed to the floor, and the woman looked embarrassed. "Rather it be here than on your fresh bed," I said to lighten the mood. "Just your water breaking, which is a good thing, my lady. It shouldn't be long now."

As soon as she was settled onto her pallet, she visibly relaxed. She looked thankful for the soft spot and closed her eyes for just a moment. "Please, call me Mary. And this is my husband, Joseph."

"Where are my manners? I'm Gertrude. My husband, Eli, and I run the inn here. It's very nice to make your acquaintance. Welcome to Bethlehem."

Mary was such a pretty young woman. She was a few years younger than me, but there was something in her eyes that made her seem older and wiser, as if she knew things about the world that the rest of us had yet to figure out. When she looked me in the eyes, I knew immediately that this was a woman I wanted to be friends with. I knew she was the type of woman to always have a kind word, and a part of me could tell that she also was in need of a good friend, especially at this particular moment in life. I could sense her apprehension at the impending birth.

I set about to preparing a place to put the baby. We didn't have much more than the trough we used to feed the animals. I took some hay and made a soft little cradle and checked the swaddling blankets over again.

"Those are beautiful," Mary said as she watched what I was doing. "Are they from your own children?" I smiled at her. "Yes and no. They were made for my children, but neither of them lived."

"I'm so sorry," Mary said before another contraction took her voice away.

Wanting to change the subject, I said, "You have more important things to focus on. The point is that God laid it in my heart to save these blankets because he knew someday a baby would have need of them, and here you are."

Joseph was quiet as he paced around the center aisle of the stable. I knew it must be hard for him. He was supposed to be protecting his wife and keeping her safe, yet they were stuck in this strange place. It was also Jewish custom that men were not allowed to be present during births. Lucky for him that I was there to help. I did what I could to ease his mind and Mary's as well.

"Joseph, why don't you go and wait outside. We will come for you when the baby arrives," I said gently, but firmly, and walked him out of the stable. I was not going to be bound by custom after seeing how concerned this father-to-be was for his wife. He would see his baby right away if he wanted to. Who was I to stop him by insisting on a rule I thought didn't recognize the father enough during the birth of their children.

"I've delivered my fair share of babies," I said to fill the silence after returning to Mary's side. "Most of them have been lambs and calves here in this stable, but I have attended many human births. The key is to remember to breathe. You know, my lady, God said he was putting enmity between us and the evil one. Childbirth was never to be easy for us after what that foolish Eve did. So just bear up. You're doing just fine. Hold on to my hands, and pull as hard as you like. There, relax while you can. This little consolation is followed by the next pain."

I held her hand while she took deep breaths. "Is this your first one?"

When the contraction subsided, Mary nodded. "Yes, he is my first child."

"He? Do you have a hunch it's a boy? I know many women who have used all kinds of tricks to try and divine what their baby will be, but I don't put much stock into. Not meaning any offense, dear, but only God knows the gifts he will give."

"No, that's all right," Mary replied. "I don't believe in any of that either. God knows how a child will turn out. My faith is in him."

I liked Mary even more. She was taking this all in stride, and her faith in God was strong, I could tell. She was like an open book, and yet there was something more to this than she was letting on. I wasn't going to push her to share more than she wanted to though. She needed to focus on delivering a healthy baby.

"I feel so sorry that the first thing your little one will see will be this old stable and these dirty animals," I said. "But at least he will be surrounded by a mother and father who love him. I must say, I am taking a liking to him myself for some odd reason, and I'm not sure why. Your baby isn't here yet, but I feel the joy already somehow."

I couldn't explain the feeling that I was having. It was much like the peace and serenity I felt when looking at that bright star earlier in the evening. It even felt similar to when I was in the midst of my prayers with God, sitting at my window having a conversation with him. I felt light and hopeful. I felt as though something spectacular was going to happen. There was the familiar feeling of anticipation and excitement again. I still couldn't explain any of it.

I peeked my head outside and saw Joseph had finally taken a seat on one of the milking stools just outside of the barn. He had his head leaned back against one of the walls, and his eyes were closed. The poor man was exhausted and had probably fallen asleep. They had a long journey to get here, so I let the him sleep for now. There would be plenty of excitement to wake him up later.

I enjoyed the peace and quiet in the barn. Even the animals were being quiet, as if they were waiting for something to happen. The only noise came from Mary shuffling around to get comfortable or breathing heavily through her contractions, which were coming closer and closer together as the night wore on.

"Oh, Gertrude," Mary suddenly cried out. "I think he's coming. Joseph, our boy is coming."

Joseph startled awake and rushed over to Mary's side disregarding the strict custom of not being at a birthing. He held her hand and helped support her up into a sitting position. I didn't interfere with his care and concern for her. Mary was breathing hard, but I could see the determination on her face as she began to push.

"I can see the baby's head. Push! You are so calm for your first time. Your face, Mary, your face! It's all glowing, like I have never seen before," I exclaimed. I couldn't believe how excited I was. I had never experienced a childbirth like this before. Mary was serene, and there appeared to be a halo of light framing her face. She looked almost divine in that moment.

But then the baby's head came out, quickly followed by the shoulders, and the rest of that tiny body. A tiny squall rang through the stable, a sure sign of life.

4

And suddenly there was a multitude of
the heavenly host with the angel,
praising God and saying:
"Glory to God in the highest,
and on earth peace
to those on whom his favor rests."

—Luke 2:13–14 (NAB)

"HOW IS HE? Is he healthy?" Mary asked immediately. Joseph had wrapped his arms around his wife's shoulders, and she leaned heavily into him.

"A baby boy!" I shouted. "Just as you said, my lady. A beautiful baby boy." I began to cry uncontrollably. I didn't know what came over me, as I hardly ever cried. I swaddled the tiny body in the blankets I had made for my own children and handed him to his mother.

"Do you hear that?" I asked. "It sounds like music. Who would be playing music this late at night? It sounds so sweet though."

The family of three looked like a tableau of perfection. There was so much joy on their faces, and the baby had already quieted down. He was just as calm and serene as his mother. Most babies were angry at being expelled into this unknown world but not Mary's little boy. He seemed observant, already taking in his surroundings. It was only moments later when Mary bared her breast and the baby boy latched on for his first nourishment.

I was so happy for this little family I had just met, but then a pang clenched my belly suddenly. Unbidden, a feeling of jealousy began to creep throughout my body. This unwelcomed thought struggled with my joy for the family. Here was this beautiful, young woman nursing her newborn, healthy son in the swaddling clothes that were meant for my children. I didn't want to feel jealous at that moment, but I couldn't help it. I tried to suppress it as tears continued to stream down my face.

"What will you name him?" I asked when the tears began to subside.

"His name is Jesus," Mary said.

"That is an interesting name. How did you decide on it?" I asked. I was determined to ignore these unjust feelings of envy toward the little family.

Mary and Joseph looked at each other. "Joseph, tell her please."

Joseph began their story. "Mary and I have not been married for very long. I had observed Mary for a long time before speaking to her father about a marriage. She was always obedient to her father and to the Lord. She always observed every law of our faith without fail. I could find no fault in her. I knew she was perfect for me. But before our marriage took place, I learned that she was pregnant. I had already learned to love her, but I struggled with this new information. I didn't want to disgrace her, so I decided that I would divorce her quietly and move on with my life."

I was shocked to my very core. I couldn't believe this of the regal woman lying before me holding her newborn son. I was entranced by their story. I knew there was more to this story, but I wasn't quite prepared for the next revelation.

"But before I could go through with the divorce, an angel of the Lord appeared to me in a dream. He said, 'Joseph, son of David, do not be afraid to take Mary your wife into your home. For it is through the Holy Spirit that this child has been conceived in her. She will bear a son and you are to name him Jesus, because he will save his people from their sins.'[1] He told me that this would fulfill the prophecy made about a child born to a virgin. It was an awesome

---

[1]   Matthew 1:20–21 (NAB)

sight, and the dream felt so real. I didn't hesitate the next morning in making sure our marriage went through. Jesus is my son, but he is truly the son of God."

I was speechless. I couldn't believe that the baby before me was the son of God. And yet, it was making sense in my mind. This was the child promised in our Scriptures to save the world. This tiny little thing, suckling from his mother, was going to be the light of the world. This was the fulfillment of the promise of a Savior I had been impatient to see realized. And here he was right before my very own eyes. Could it be really he?

They were so happy together, and Joseph looked on baby Jesus as though he were his own. The pride in his eyes was unmatched by any other father I had ever encountered. Surely this was all Yahweh's doing. I was speechless. When I finally found my voice, all I could say was, "I will let you rest, but I'll be out in the morning to bring you your breakfast. Please get some rest, Mary." I held her hand for a moment and squeezed.

"Thank you, Gertrude, for everything you have done for us."

"Thank you for coming into my life," I replied, still feeling a loss for words.

I left the new family alone in the barn and made my way into the main house, my mind swimming of thoughts of what I had just witnessed and the story I'd just heard. The climb up the stairs was the hardest it had ever been. Now that I was alone, I was alone with my thoughts. God had indeed answered my prayer for a child to make use of those blankets, but he had not answered my prayer the way I had intended it. All my life I had dreamed of having a family of my own, but two stillborn babies were a crushing blow. They were in my thoughts always. I found myself thinking about what kind of young men they would have been had they survived. I wasn't used to being jealous of anyone before, and I didn't like the way it ate at my joy for this new mother. Thankfully, the bedroom offered me a bit of solace as I observed Eli snoring peacefully, and I fell gratefully into my bed. I prayed that night that God would help me to conquer my feelings of jealousy—this was God's very own son—if Joseph's story was to be believed. How could I be jealous of God's son? *Help me, Lord, to stand faithful in the midst of this storm of envy.*

I woke to my husband calling my name and shaking me awake. I had slept so soundly and so deeply that I didn't even notice when the sun came up. The morning meal was being prepared as I came downstairs. I immediately remembered my charges out in the stable. I began to gather a hearty breakfast for them. Mary would especially need to keep her strength up in order to feed her child.

"Where were you all night?" my husband asked as I carried my basket of food to the door.

"I was in the stable with our guests. The lady had her baby last night. A beautiful baby boy."

"Are they okay? Do they need anything?" he asked.

It warmed my heart to see the concern on his face. There was even a glimmer of remorse for having delegated them to such poor housing. "No, my dear. They want for nothing. I'm taking them breakfast right now."

The morning was beautiful, and the sky was clear. The weather was perfect. Bethlehem was already bustling with life, but it was quiet in the back near our stable. This time I knocked on the stable wall to announce my presence before letting myself in.

I found them all huddled together in the little stall. Joseph was holding baby Jesus in his arms while Mary looked on. She looked surprisingly relaxed and rested. After her ordeal yesterday, I assumed she would be sleeping every chance she had, but there she was just watching her two favorite men. There seemed to be no concern for the Jewish customs; I could see that mother and father had already begun to parent the blessed child given to them by God.

"You look very well, my lady," I said as I began to lay out the breakfast of dried dates, figs, nuts, fruit, fresh bread, and honey and cool water from our well.

"Please, Gertrude, just call me Mary. I am nobody special."

"Well, we can agree to disagree on that aspect, but if you like, I shall call you Mary."

"Thank you."

I began to pass out food to the new parents, who had hearty appetites. I couldn't imagine the long and difficult journey to Bethlehem and the burden that now rested on their shoulders. I was in turmoil myself as the jealousy and joy for this family fought for my attention. It was a strange feeling, to be sure, but the more I watched the baby, the more joy won out and peace began to settle over me. I had so much work to do that day. We had a couple of guests leaving the inn, so I would need to gather their bedsheets for washing and scrub that room clean. I knew the sitting room needed to be spruced up, and the list went on and on, but there in the stable I knew that the day would work itself out.

Once they had finished their meal, I had to excuse myself because I really did have work to attend to. As much as I wanted to sit in the stable and watch the baby sleep while his parents adored him, I had other guests who needed me as well. But my tasks didn't seem burdensome because I told myself that once I was done with my chores that I could go back outside and see that little boy once more. It would be my reward for a job well done. I vowed not let an old, impatient attitude affect how I would go about my chores for the day.

So I set about cleaning and helping with the cooking. I even took the time to double-check my husband's math and take a quick inventory of our stock before the new stores showed up later that afternoon. It was amazing the amount of work I was able to accomplish that day. Most days I drudged through my work as if it was a burden. I didn't always take enjoyment in my tasks but rather saw them as something necessary I had to do in order to live. We had to make money in order to eat and keep ourselves clothed, but I never considered that one day cleaning bedrooms and washing sheets would bring me happiness. This day found my spirit light and joyful.

The joy in my heart that day was obvious. It even seemed to be contagious as I noticed my husband was also in a good mood. I couldn't attribute it all to the nice profit we had turned over the last few weeks; I knew some of it had to come from me. He could see the joy in my heart and just couldn't keep a scowl on around me. Eli and I had always been able to discern each other's mood and reflect it back. The other guests also seemed happier. Yesterday they were complaining about the census and the tax that King Herod was collecting to fill his coffers, but today, they seemed glad and joyous to be alive.

Then I started to wonder if it was all coming from more than just my good mood as I continuously looked out of the window toward the stable. Maybe this joyous feeling was coming from someone else. Maybe all of my guests could sense the presence of this little miracle baby outside in that lowly stable.

As soon as I had completed my tasks, I raced out to the stable, to get another glimpse of the child. My envious thoughts had all but disappeared. At first I had wondered why God would bless this couple and not my husband and me. Were we not devoted enough to him? Were we not deserving of a child to love? But as the day progressed, my mood had lifted, and I was eager again to be with this family. I knew the couple would be staying with us for at least forty days for her purification before traveling back to their home. I wanted to spend as much time with my newfound friend, Mary; her husband, Joseph; and baby Jesus as I possibly could.

I found Mary was again awake. Joseph had left for a time, going to the city officials to be counted in the census. Mary told me that he left to go pay his taxes and be counted, so I decided to stay with Mary till he returned. The baby was wide awake and was already fed, so he was content to watch the world. With grace and ease, Mary wrapped her baby snuggly in the swaddling clothes I'd given her. She looked at me for a long while. We shared a moment of intimacy, of friendship that I had prayed for, longed for many years. I knew that finally God had answered my prayers.

"Would you like to hold him?" Mary asked, lifting her baby and proffering him to me.

5

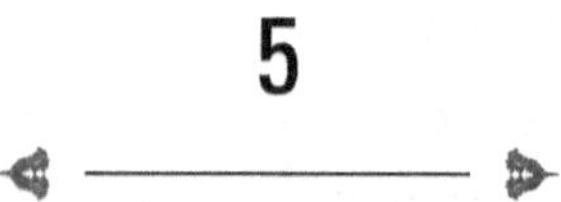

*When the angels went away from them to heaven,
the shepherds said to one another,
"Let's go, then, to Bethlehem and see
this thing that has taken place,
which the Lord has made known to us."
So they went in haste and found Mary and Joseph,
and the infant lying in the manger.*

—Luke 2:15–16 (NAB)

IT WAS A simple question, "Would you like to hold him?" Normally, I would never have hesitated to hold a baby, but this time was different. It seemed as though there was so much more to that question than a simple offer for me to hold her son. I couldn't explain it in the moment, but it was as though by accepting the offer to hold this child meant that I was accepting him into my heart. He had already found a small spot in there, as all children I encountered did. But this child was different. Special. Could this baby heal my heart, wounded for so long since the loss of my own babies? Could I accept what this mother was offering as she offered her son to me?

I was beginning to believe that this child was more than just another baby born in our inn. He was the future—and not just a future generation but eternity. That was the kind of commitment holding him felt like, that I had to commit to an eternity of loving him. It was a daunting task for anyone to consider, but I realized that Mary and Joseph had committed to loving him and raising him as their own. Could I love him too?

"Yes, I will," I said out loud and held out my arms.

Mary nodded and handed baby Jesus over to me, and I could tell by her expression that she knew what I was accepting. She knew that I wasn't just agreeing to hold her child in my arms for a moment but to hold him in my heart for my lifetime. I looked into Mary's eyes as I took the child and held him close to my heart. What passed between us remained unspoken yet understood. Our hearts were united in love with this child.

The weight of Jesus in my arms was light. He looked at me with clear eyes as though he recognized me from when I delivered him. His gaze was unwavering as I stroked his cheek with my finger and touched his tiny hand. "Ten little fingers and ten little toes," I said. "You are perfection." His little hand reached out and grasped my finger. "Oh what strength you already have. You are going to be so strong one day. You are truly a blessed little child."

I watched him for so long, and I could see that the exhaustion was starting to catch up to Mary. "Why don't you sleep? I'll stay and watch the baby right here and wake you if he needs anything at all. Be at peace, my lady, Mary."

Mary lay down in the hay and immediately fell asleep. I sat in the quiet warmth of the stable and rocked Jesus in my arms. He watched me the whole time, and his eyes twinkled when I began to sing little hymns to him. It was never too early to learn the joy that comes from Yahweh. The time I spent with this baby boy was a reminder of the two children I never got to hold and nurture. But the sorrow of those losses was replaced with love and hope that one day I would see my own babies again. Could it be that this little boy was the Savior, the Messiah, foretold by our ancestors? My heart soared with joy. I felt the sorrow of my own loss turn to a joy, a love that I could hardly contain. My tears renewed my spirit.

Joseph arrived just before dinner, and Mary woke and began to nurse Jesus. I went into the house and brought out food once again and spent time sharing the evening meal with the couple. They shared stories with me about where they grew up and their life at home while I shared my experiences as an innkeeper's wife and the various people I had encountered coming through our inn. I told them about some of the people I'd met who were demanding, rude, and inconsiderate of the people who served them. The self-ishness of some people who had stayed in our inn always made me angry. I often was impatient with those whose only interest was their own needs. Patience and mercy were not easy virtues for me.

It became obvious through each of our stories that we all understood just how much the world needed a savior. They shared their fear of how quickly the people arose to stone Mary when her pregnancy was revealed. The people were quick to anger and showed no compassion for the young girl, insisting on following the letter of the law.

Night began to fall, and I knew I should let them rest. It still seemed bright outside because that one star was high in the sky, sitting just above Bethlehem. I was about to excuse myself when a knock came to the stable door. I went to open it, assuming it was my husband looking for me or perhaps a guest needing to have his horse sad-dled. Instead, three men stood before me. They were richly dressed in robes of bright colors and sumptuous fabrics. They all wore beards and had fine sandals strapped to their feet. Three camels were tied to a post just outside of the stable. I had never seen such men as these, dressed with such finery.

"Can I help you?" I asked a bit wary. It was much too late in the evening for visitors.

"Is this where we can find the king of the Jews?" one asked. He had gray hair, almost turning white. The other two men stood beside him.

"I'm sorry? I don't understand."

A second one with dark-brown hair spoke next. "We have traveled a long way, following the star overhead." He pointed to the sky where that bright star twinkled. "The prophecy foretold of the Messiah being born here, and the star has guided our way. We would like to see the infant king."

They knew about Jesus. I didn't know what else to do but to let them in. I showed them where Mary and Joseph were sitting with Jesus. As soon as the three men saw the baby, they each fell to their knees and bowed their heads.

Joseph looked stunned, but Mary had a serene look in her eyes as if she had expected this.

"We have come to worship the Messiah," the white-haired man said.

Then they each placed an ornate box in front of Mary and offered gifts to Jesus. In each box there was gold, frankincense, or myrrh. They said prayers over him and threw up their thanks to God for blessing the world with his son. Soon they began to tell their tale about their lives as magi and how they had been waiting for this day. They had studied the prophecies foretold in the scriptures carefully; they knew God would keep his promise to the world and had traveled a great distance to witness it. When the star appeared in the sky, they knew they would find the king of the Jews. They explained how they had visited King Herod, assuming he would know exactly where to find the Messiah, but the King didn't know. Herod had dispatched them to find Jesus and report back, but their duty was to God only. They only wanted to worship Jesus and to present their gifts, deciding not to return any news to Herod.

"We will not disturb you any longer," the brown-haired man said. The third man remained silent.

"It's no trouble," Joseph said. "We thank you for the gifts and wish you well on your journey. Where will you go?"

"We will go and spread the word that a savior has come. The world must know of his birth so that they will know him when he is grown. He will save us all one day, and the world must prepare to make room for him in their hearts."

I watched all of this in awe. I couldn't believe that I was a witness to it all. They had called Jesus the Messiah. Could that really be true? The three men said their good-byes and set out in the night. I too had to make my own exit finally. I had a lot to process from the day, and I was eager to share this great news with my husband.

6

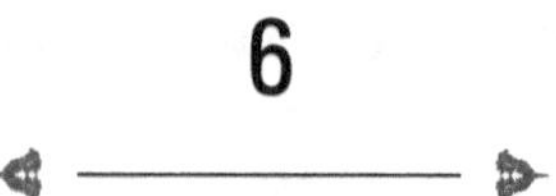

—Matthew 2: 13–14 (NAB)

I WOKE UP as normal the next day. I was still tired but not so exhausted that I didn't miss the start of a new day. I couldn't wait to find the time to talk to my Eli about the miracle sleeping out in our stable. It seemed strange to me that so much had changed in my life in just two days, and my husband had no idea that something had even happened. He sensed my good mood and didn't question its source.

For the next several weeks, I spent as much time as possible with my new family. Mary and I talked about many things. She explained to me about the message given to her from an angel that she would conceive and the child would be a boy.

I questioned her a great deal, my curiosity getting the better of me. I asked how her faith in God could be so absolute and unwavering. How was she able to say yes to the angel when she knew what it might cost her, to be pregnant and unmarried? She inspired me to stop my own doubting and questioning God about why he allowed so much evil, corruption, and sin in the world. While running the inn, I had seen my share of the worst in people. I decided right then that I wanted to have her kind of faith in God. I wanted the courage to stand faithful even though I might be stoned. I placed my trust in her and in turn received a greater faith in the God who gave her the courage to say yes. I asked him for the same courage.

It was getting closer to the end of Mary's time of purification. Her son had been circumcised and given the name Yeshewa, Jesus. I knew their time with us was coming to an end. They were bound to return to their home. I did not want to think of that day.

Like many mornings, I gathered up breakfast and went to the stable to see Mary, Joseph, and Jesus. I knew that they wouldn't be staying long now that their task of paying taxes and registering with the census was done. I wondered if they would soon leave for Nazareth.

When I arrived at the stable, their things were all gathered up. "Mary?" I called. "Are you still here?"

"Oh, yes, Gertrude, we are still here. I must tell you, we are leaving today," Mary said as she came from the animal side of the stable. Joseph led their donkey out, which was now laden with all their belongings, including the gifts the wise men had given them. He seemed very anxious to get started.

"Is something wrong? Is it the baby?" I asked frantically.

Mary gave a small laugh. "No, Jesus is perfectly fine. He's sleeping right now."

"Then what's the matter? Why the hurry?"

"I had another dream last night," Joseph said. "I had another vision from God who told us to leave this place and not delay."

"Why would he want you to leave so quickly? Mary should rest for a few more days before beginning a long journey. You know that donkey isn't very comfortable."

"An angel of the Lord appeared to me and said, 'Rise, take the child and his mother, flee to Egypt, and stay there until I tell you. Herod is going to search for the child to destroy him."[1] The magi didn't return to the king like he had ordered them to. The king is angered by this betrayal, and his vengeance will be mighty. We must flee before his soldiers can find us."

I couldn't believe what I was hearing. Baby Jesus was in danger. I didn't want my new friends to leave me, and Egypt was so very far away. I feared that I would never see them again. Mary saw the despair in my eyes and gave me an enveloping hug. I had just found an answer to my prayers in her, and now she was leaving just as our friendship was growing. She held me for a second as I tried not to cry.

"Why do you have to go to Egypt? Why not back home to Nazareth?" I asked.

"Because Herod will be able to find us there," Joseph explained. "Since I have registered for the census, he will know where we live and that we have a newborn son. We must get out of his reach."

I wiped my tears and wanted to be strong. I knew in my heart that my burden of losing a friend was much less than the burden Mary and Joseph carried with needing to protect their son. "Give me a moment, and I will get some food for you. It will be a long journey."

---

[1] Matthew 2:13 (NAB)

I ran into the house. My husband tried to stop me to ask a question, but I flew by him without so much as a second glance. He was accustomed to my spontaneous decision to help someone who I thought in need and knew it was no use trying to slow me down. Once I had an idea, there was no stopping me. He just smiled and went back to his ledgers.

I ordered the cook to gather food for a long journey and then ran up to my room. I dug in my dresser, deep in the back of the bottom drawer, and pulled out a small leather pouch. I shook it and heard coins jingle together. It wasn't much money, but it was all I had put away on my own. My husband knew I kept my little treasure from the sale of my weavings. I would explain to him all about where the money went later; right now, I had to hurry.

I grabbed the food from the kitchen and took it to the stable. Joseph had everything ready to go and was waiting on me. He tried to protest when I shoved the money into his hands, but I insisted. "Take care of yourself and your family? I will see you all again someday." I had no idea of when that might be or how I thought it possible. It came out of my mouth without my even thinking about it.

Mary handed Jesus to me once more. I gave him one last squeeze and kissed his forehead. "Good-bye, my king. You will always live in my heart."

Then I hugged Mary again. I held on for a long time as I hugged her close. She had already endured the journey here pregnant, and now she had to endure a longer journey with a newborn. I couldn't even imagine. But she was a strong woman, and if anybody could do this, it was her.

"I feel as if I've known you my whole life," I admitted.

"I feel the same," she said. "You will always be my friend, Gertrude, and I wish you all God's blessings. May he keep you all safe!"

"I'll pray to God for your safe journey and that we meet again, whether it be here on earth or in heaven someday."

"Amen," she said. Then Joseph helped her up onto the donkey, and I handed her the baby still swaddled in my child's blankets.

I couldn't stop the tears as I waved good-bye and watched them walk away into the late hours of the afternoon. Why did I find a friend with whom I felt such a profound connection and then lose her? Our friendship was just beginning to grow. Would we ever meet again? I prayed it would be so but really could not see it to be possible.

Finally, when I lost sight of them, I turned and walked back to the inn that felt much emptier. My chores were no longer inviting, and Eli could instantly tell something was wrong. I tried to explain as best I could about Mary and Joseph and the connection I felt with them.

"God will hear your prayers, and you will see them again," Eli said as he hugged me gently. He was always able to make me feel better and said just what I needed to hear, even though my doubts still persisted.

I wiped the tears from my eyes and said, "There's more to it, husband."

Eli leaned back. "What do you mean?"

"I felt such a strong connection to their son. It feels as though I'm losing my children all over again."

I watched Eli as the emotions played over his face. I could see the hurt and sorrow he still felt for our boys, and I suddenly felt incredibly sad that Eli never met Jesus before the family had to flee. It seemed like he was missing out on something incredible.

Eli and I sat together for a long while as I told him their incredible story and of my experience when I first held their baby boy. I explained to him my feelings of jealousy and then of love for his child. I told him I did not understand it all but knew that this family would play a significant part of our lives somehow. Eli listened intently to my telling.

"Gerty, I have also trusted your instincts about things. You seem to always be able to read the heart of people. I'm sure if what you believe about these people is true, God will reveal it to be so. For now let us just be content to enjoy their stay and wait on the Lord's plan to unfold."

I was satisfied with his answer and was relieved he didn't think I had lost my mind. I was indeed content to wait on the Lord to reveal his plans for my family and the family of my new friend, Mary.

"These three men also came and said that Jesus was to be the Messiah," I added, voicing my own confusion and doubt.

"Hmm," was all the reply he gave to that.

"What do you think, husband? Could it be true?"

"Pray on it," he said simply. "God will show you the truth."

7

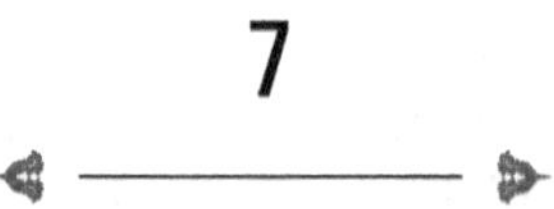

—Matthew 3:16–18 (NAB)

ELI WAS UP before sunrise the next morning, so we didn't have a chance to talk about yesterday's events. He was busy with our guests when I came downstairs to start my day. He was more pensive than normal, and I knew he was still thinking about what we had discussed the night before. I didn't want to pressure him just yet. I was still confused as well. I had prayed to God, and he hadn't answered me yet. I didn't feel any overwhelming knowledge one way or the other.

I knew he needed time to process everything. My impatience was getting the better of me as usual. But in the meantime, I had work and chores to get to. Many of the guests were leaving that day, though a few had decided to linger and wait for the crowds to thin out before heading home again. It was a bittersweet time because I liked having a full house; although, I would not miss the added workload. I was reminded that my new friend Mary was gone with her precious son.

Things were quiet around the inn as I cleaned out the vacant rooms and gathered the linens to wash. I took them out to the back of the yard to wash and hang in the breeze. Something felt strange as I submerged my hands in the warm water and scrubbed soap into the dirty laundry. Bethlehem was a noisy place, to be sure, but today's noises just seemed odd, like a jarring note in an otherwise soothing lullaby. I tried to push it from my mind but— *Was that a cry?* I thought. *What is all that shouting I hear?*

My hands stopped working as I strained to hear, but all I could hear were carts on the street, a donkey braying, and some merchant trying to sell his wares. I shook my head and chided myself. *Making up stories again, Gerty. You're acting as high strung as a cat in a thunderstorm.*

I finished washing and hanging all of the laundry, but things still did not feel right. I went to cooking area where the normally talkative cook was quiet as she kneaded her bread, exchanging only the briefest of greetings. Eli had gone into town to take care of some business. Our groceries still had not been delivered, so Eli decided it was worth a trip for him to talk to our supplier rather than wait until we were completely out of everything.

I was sitting in the front room double-checking all of our ledgers, including what we had in stock for supplies and food. We were definitely running low on so much, but if the books were correct, we had done quite well over the past months of the census.

Suddenly, the front door banged open, and I jumped from my seat in fright. Eli stood there panting, having run all the way from the market. One of the guests who had decided to stay around came rushing in after Eli. They closed the door behind them before both men fell into their seats.

"Good heavens!" I exclaimed. "What has happened?"

All the guest could do was point out toward the city while trying to catch his breath. But Eli sat up straight and took a deep breath. "There are soldiers swarming into the city," he said.

My first thought was that Eli had gotten into some sort of argument with the grocer, but Eli was so even tempered that I couldn't think anything he could get in trouble for. I had never known him to even raise his voice, let alone hit a man, but something had clearly frightened these two men.

"What do they want?" I asked, afraid of the answer.

Eli looked at me levelly. "King Herod has sent out a proclamation and is rounding up all little boys two and under. They say he wants to find the King. Gertrude, it must all be true, everything you told me about the baby—it must be!" I could hear the fear in his voice.

My hand flew to my mouth as I tried not to cry out. Joseph's words of warning came back to my mind, and I knew they were searching for Jesus. I sat there and prayed to God that Mary and Joseph were far enough away by now. Herod hadn't wasted any time, but the precious little family had a full day's head start on the soldiers. *Dear Lord, let this be enough time for them to get away.*

"It's chaos in the city," the man finally spoke up. "I want to leave as quickly as possible. There's no telling what the soldiers will do if they don't find who they are looking for."

"Yes, yes. I understand." I stood up and smoothed down my skirt as the man raced upstairs to gather his things. But Eli had stayed seated. He was staring into the fireplace with a look I knew only too well. He was contemplating something.

"Gertrude, will you help this man settle his account, please?" Eli stood up and looked at me soberly.

"Of course. What are you going to do?"

"I'm going to go next door and make sure Laban and Rebecca's baby is hidden and remains safe. I know that Laban is normally at work in the fields at this time of day and—"

I cut him off. "Yes, go quickly," I urged. "Yes, Eli, go and help them, and I will take care of things here. Maybe you could help Rebecca hide young Caleb behind one of the stalls in the stable. The soldiers may not look there for any children. What do I do if the soldiers come?"

"You will let them in. And, Gerty please, don't speak directly to them. Be polite, answer their questions, and nothing more." He spread his hands out wide. We don't have any children here, so there's no fear. I would never ask you to lie, but if they ask about any other children, don't tell them about Laban and Rebecca's little boy, Caleb."

"I won't. Eli, please be safe."

I kissed him gently. It wasn't the normal swift peck I gave him in the morning or at night but a kiss I tried to put all of my feelings into. Eli held his hand to my cheek and gently brushed a tear away with his thumb.

"I will, Gerty. I'll be back as soon as I can."

He left right as the guest came rushing down the stairs. We settled his account quickly, and he left the inn. I paced from window to window, hoping to see Eli returning home.

I wanted to be with him and help him to protect our neighbors and their infant boy.

Eventually, I went up to the top floor and pulled out my prayer journal. I sat on the bench in front of the window and looked out over Bethlehem. It looked peaceful from up here. I flipped through the pages and read some of my previous prayers and began to calm down. There were so many comforting words written. I came across a prayer that I wrote down specifically for anxious times. They were like a salve for my soul. I couldn't quite gather my thoughts enough to make a new prayer, so I took solace in reciting my old ones.

My peace was broken when I began to hear screams. The high-pitched wailing of women pierced the air. I shuddered to think of what could be happening. We were told that the soldiers were gathering up all the children under two years. Once they determined that none of them were the King, they would leave our city.

But these screams increased in number and intensity. *Where was Eli? Why hasn't he returned yet?* Something wasn't right. I could feel a growing sense of dread. Unable to stay inside, I went downstairs, grabbed my shawl, which was hanging on a peg just inside the front door, wrapped it tightly around my shoulders, and stepped out into the evening air. The screaming and wailing seemed to be coming from every household. *What could be happening?*

I heard the hooves coming up our street and saw the solders stride right into Laban and Rebecca's home, and coming out, they rounded the house and strode toward the stables. I stood in horror. *Please don't let them find Caleb.* As the first soldier emerged from the side of the house, Rebecca was running after him, screaming, "Please, please, don't hurt him."

Just then, he tossed the small body at her. She caught her baby boy and fell to the ground. The last soldier kicked her aside as they galloped down the street and headed right into another household. I ran to Rebecca, clutching her dead baby; his blanket already soaked crimson from the gaping chest wound.

"How could they do this? How could they? My baby, my baby!" Then it seemed she recognized who I was and grabbed my hands. "I'm so sorry, Gertrude, he tried to protect my son. Your Eli was so brave, but they were stronger than him."

I looked up into the house, unsure of her meaning. I slowly rose and went to the front door. The soldiers had overturned everything. Then, barely, I could hear the faint rasp of a breath. I followed the sound to the back of the house. There was Eli, sitting against the doorjamb. He was sitting up, but his face was ghostly white. He had his hand pressed into his stomach, and I could see the red glint of blood seeping between his fingers with every labored breath he took.

"Eli," I gasped and fell to my knees. "What happened?"

He looked up at me. "The soldiers came," he managed to say though I could see the toll it was taking for him to speak. I tried to press my hands to his wound to stop the bleeding, but I knew I was too late. I could see the large wound in his stomach. "I tried to hide the boy, but they found him. I tried to stop them, Gerty, I tried. They took the boy. What evil is being done to these innocents, such evil?"

"Eli, just breathe and relax. Everything is going to be all right." The tears were coming hard and fast now. They seemed to burn their way down my cheeks and splashed onto my bloodied hands.

"Gerty, you are right, it will be all right. Now, just listen." He held my gaze, and his voice was becoming fainter with every word. "The soldiers may come back. You need to get away. Go, follow Mary and Joseph. Find our Messiah. You will be safe with them."

I almost fell backward. Of all the things he could've said, I never would have expected him to be talking about my friends.

"That child is the one Herod is after. That child must be the Messiah, and you need to find him. Gerty, promise me that you will follow the true King." He held my hand firmly.

"I promise," I said quickly. I didn't fully realize what I was promising, but I would have promised him anything.

"I love you." He put his hand back up to my cheek, and I held it there. "You have been the best wife I could have ever hoped for. You kept me faithful when I was weak. Your faith has never wavered and was strong enough for both of us. Live for yourself now. Live for our King because he is the savior. Promise me you will find them. "

"I will. Oh, Eli, I love you so much. Please don't leave me."

I leaned forward and kissed Eli on the lips. I brushed the hair from his forehead and looked him in the eyes. I knew the moment he had passed. He looked beyond me to something far greater and smiled. I knew that smile was for the Lord as he greeted my husband into his loving arms. I held Eli in my arms and cried for yet another loss. How great was my pain. I couldn't move, paralyzed with grief. What would I do without my husband, my Eli? I realized with a whisper of wisdom that Eli was with our babies. He and our boys were together.

As though something invisible pulled me up, I stood and made my way home. In a daze, I wandered up to our small apartment at the top of the stairs. It seemed so empty and lonely now. I was a widow. The thought seemed to slap me, breaking me into a million pieces. This morning, I was married and happy; now I was widowed and devastated. What was I to do?

I sat in my chair near the window. My tears came, shaking me. I wanted to die and be with Eli and our babies. I didn't want to go on without them. My life had forever changed in an instant. I was alone. I prayed, *Lord God why have you done this to me? How can I survive without Eli? Haven't you taken enough from me already?* All my strength sapped; I gave in to my anger, fell to my knees, and railed at God. *Why, why, why have you done this to me?*

After a long while in silence, I looked around the little room I shared with Eli for so many years, the bed we shared and the meager belongings we had. His robe and bed clothes were still lying on the shelf near the washbasin. My heart broke with grief that I would never share this space with my Eli again. I knew with certainty that I couldn't stay there. The truth came to me as a soft whisper that was familiar. There was no way I could live here and run the inn. And besides, I had made my promise to Eli to follow Mary and Joseph. It would be no easy task to find them. All I knew was that they were headed to Egypt, and I didn't even know the way. Could I find them?

I'd never get anywhere if I didn't try. I washed the blood from my hands and discarded the soiled dress I was wearing. There was no saving it from the blood that had soaked through the fabric. I could never wear it again anyway. I gathered my things together and made a plan to set out the next day. I was exhausted. I lay in my bed alone. *Lord God, if it is your will for me to find my friend Mary and her husband, Joseph, you must show me the way.*

I needed to do something about the inn. I couldn't just completely abandon it. We employed several men who were honest, hard workers that I knew to be trustworthy until the owner could hire a new manager. I was able to finally drift to sleep with a plan in mind.

Early the next morning, two of the men who worked closely with Eli came to tell me that Laban had asked them to come and prepare little Caleb's and Eli's bodies for burial. I was overwhelmed with gratitude. I thanked them and joined the procession of friends and workers from our inn to Eli's burial. I allowed my tears to flow freely, fully and running over. I allowed them to do their work in my soul, in my heart, comforting me, healing my pain, and giving me strength to go on.

After spending a long time at the grave of my beloved Eli, I went back to the inn for the last time. I gathered my meager belongings in a travel bag and placed my prayer journal on top. I found our savings tucked under the mattress and added that to my bag as well. I even gathered as many weaving and sewing supplies as I could. I would take our donkey for the journey so I could take most my supplies. I gathered up food and water for several days. It all sounded like a good plan. How could I leave my Eli? I stopped in our room, sat on the bed, and prayed.

Oh, God, please help me to do this. Help me to find them.

I strapped everything securely to the donkey and made my way through town. I had asked one of the travelers for some basic directions that would get me on the path to Egypt. I had no idea how far it was. All I knew was that I had to go and was counting on God to show me the way. I stopped in front of our inn for a long good-bye—to our inn, to my beloved Eli, to my babies, and to the only life I'd known.

8

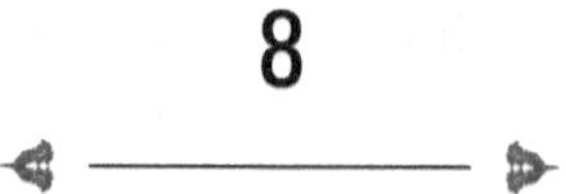

—Matthew 5:3–4 (NAB)

MARY, JOSEPH, AND their son, Jesus, my Messiah, had a two-day start on me, but I hoped that since I was traveling alone, I could catch up. I wondered whether or not they would stay on the main road, or if they would try to take some lesser known paths. If they had gone that way, then I knew this would be like finding a needle in a haystack. All I could do was pray that God would show me the right way. I felt him calling me to embark on this journey, so I decided to trust his guidance. I would follow Mary's example and stand faithful to him. I had nothing else left. Now I counted on him to stand faithful to me in return.

The first night I stopped at a small but well-kept inn. I asked the clerk behind the front desk if he had seen a young couple with a newborn baby come through. I had been scared to ask too much because I knew Herod might still be sending out his soldiers to hunt down more baby boys, and I didn't want to draw any suspicions on them. The clerk seemed very nice.

"Oh, yes. I had a family leave just this morning. They had the most adorable baby boy with them. He seemed to be content to watch the world from his mother's arms. And his eyes…he seemed to look right through me. I was surprised to learn he was only a few months old."

A smile spread across my face. That was my little Jesus for sure. The clerk described his demeanor exactly. "Thank you. I'll take a room for one night please," I said with a huge grin on my face. I could rest easy that night knowing that I was on the right path and that I was close to meeting up with them. I knew then that the Lord was surely guiding my way. Although my pain of losing Eli was so deep, I did feel a glimmer of hope that I might survive this. I vowed to find the guts to continue. I reminded God once again to stand faithful to me.

The next morning, I was up early and ready to go. I had a quick breakfast before I got on my way. I received many strange stares as I traveled down the road. I assumed it was uncommon to see a woman traveling alone, and it occurred to me that there might be thieves and robbers along the way looking to take advantage. There were a few times when I passed groups of men who looked hardened from their daily lives. They would eye me and the goods I carried, but I made sure to eye them back. I didn't want to give anyone the chance to think I was some weak woman they could easily overtake. I wanted every person I passed to know that I was someone to contend with. And not only that, but I knew I had God watching over me, so each time those eyes just slid on past me and focused on the road ahead.

It was around midday that I saw figures in the distance. It was hard to tell, but it looked like a man leading a donkey with someone seated on top. I urged my own donkey to hurry on. I was poised to overtake them just as they were stopping for lunch.

I rode up slowly because I did not want to frighten them, but as usual, my excitement got the better of me, and I practically ran to greet them.

"Gertrude?" Mary asked in surprise when she saw my face. "What are you doing here? How did you find us?"

"Oh, Mary!" I cried. "I'm so glad I found you all safe!"

"Sit, sit," Joseph urged. "Take a rest and tell us how you come to be here. We are preparing for our noon meal. You will eat with us."

I took his words and sat down next to Mary, who had just begun to nurse the precious child. I remembered that she always fed her son before she ate any meal.

I couldn't help but feel joy in spite of my grief-stricken heart. I felt so comfortable again being near this family. Joseph began to pass out some food, and I took out my water to share. I had felt so hurried to catch up to them, and now I felt as though I could relax. I'm sure they were still anxious to put more distance between themselves and King Herod, but I knew now that everything was going to be okay.

"Please, tell us what happened, Gertrude," Mary said, still looking at me in surprise.

I told them about Herod's men coming to Bethlehem and rounding up all of the boys under the age of two. "He is such an evil man. He didn't leave a single baby boy alive," I added with a frown, tears flowing again. "It was terrible. The mothers and fathers are despairing the loss of their children. Oh, Mary, Joseph, I pray that God will comfort them somehow, but I cannot imagine any relief from such a terrible tragedy."

Then I had to tell them about Eli and the promise I made him. "Mary, he accepted your little boy as his Messiah. He believed me when I told him about you and Joseph and this precious baby. In his dying breath, he told me to find you and then live for our newfound King."

Mary and Joseph didn't say anything for a long moment. Mary put her arm around me, and I felt the warmth and love resonating from her. "Gertrude, I am so sorry for what you have been through and lost. I know how much you loved your husband and enjoyed working at the inn." Her touch comforted me somehow. I knew now Eli was enjoying his eternity with our Lord. Mary and Joseph knew that as well. So we sat in companionable silence for a long while as we all watched Jesus yawn and fall asleep.

As we were finishing our midday meal, I broke the silence. "I want to come with you," I said bluntly.

"What about your family in Bethlehem and the inn?" Mary asked. "Won't they miss you?"

"Bethlehem was Eli's home, and the family remaining there are his people. I have some relatives who live in Cana, but now my heart belongs near you, Joseph, and this little one," I said sincerely.

"We can't promise that this will be an easy journey. Gertrude, if you are willing to endure difficulty, work hard, and be changed, you are welcomed to come with us," Mary said. I knew she wasn't just talking about the trek to Egypt.

"Mary, you know what I have been through, you know me better than anyone besides my dear Eli. You know all I've lost. I have come to love you and Joseph and especially your little Jesus. The life I used to have is no more. I have to make a new life for myself, and I would like you and your family to be part of it. I am willing to be your servant if that is what you need of me. I'm not looking for an easy life, and I've never been afraid of working hard," I said, not sure of exactly what type of change she expected of me. I would have done anything for her and was eager to agree.

Well, I'm glad you aren't afraid of hard work Gertrude because there will be plenty of it, and Mary will surely need your help. I'm really happy you are coming along with us. Welcome to our family." Joseph started as he stood and stretched. "I guess we better keep going then. We're almost to our new home in Egypt."

My heart was lighter as we packed up our things and headed back on the road. This was the beginning of the rest of my life, and I was anxious to see how it would unfold.

As we rode toward Egypt, I prayed that God would reveal to me the purpose for all that had happened to me. *Why couldn't Eli and I come with Mary and Joseph to Egypt?* I knew he would never have left Bethlehem and the inn. He grew up there and would never leave his home. I wanted to follow this boy King and felt a strong sense of anticipation for the future with him.

As I prayed, I heard that familiar whisper again, *Gertrude, I know you loved Eli. Sometimes I must remove an obstacle in order for my children to fulfill their destiny. Your purpose is unfolding. Stand faithful, my daughter, and continue to pray big as you always have.*

I felt my heart expand and knew I had made the right decision to leave Bethlehem after all. We traveled easily for several more days without incident.

We settled easily in a small village near Alexandria, knowing that King Herod's power couldn't reach us there. The threat and worry over little Jesus's life was lifted, and we were all ready for a fresh new start. We found a house near the edge of the village where the four of us could live in peace. Joseph found work quickly doing carpentry. I lived in a small cottage near the rear of their house. I thought it was important for the young couple to have their own space. I still was grieving the death of Eli and needed time alone as well.

I worked on my weaving, thankful to have brought along all of my supplies. The rhythm of weaving my favorite patterns came back to my fingertips easily. I knew this was a God-given talent I didn't want to squander. God had given me the ability to make the swaddling clothes for Jesus, and I knew now there was more that these fingers could do. I soon found a merchant willing to buy my cloth, which allowed me to contribute to the family.

I also took it upon myself to do most of the shopping. I had a sharp tongue and loved to haggle with the other merchants. It made me feel like Eli was there with me when we were running the inn. It seemed insignificant in the long run, but I always felt some pride in saving a little bit of money. Eli always praised this talent of mine. When I came home with my money pouch still jangling, he would kiss me and say, "That's my Gerty. I think you sometimes just surprise people out of their goods with your quick tongue."

The time I wasn't weaving was spent with Mary and her little boy. I helped with the cooking and cleaning mostly. We even started a small herb garden. I felt like it was my duty to earn my keep with them. Even though I lived in my own little house, I felt like I was becoming a part of the family and wanted to do my part. They had been so kind to let me come along and to share their lives with me. I didn't want to become a burden. I have always been an independent woman even when married to Eli. It is what kept him always having to remind me that women are to be submissive to their husbands (unless I was saving him money) and that I rebelled against. I wanted our marriage to be more of a partnership between two loving companions. We eventually found common ground and had a fulfilling relationship. Eli knew when to put his foot down, and I learned when not to resist. God had much to do with that lesson.

My friendship with Mary grew steadily. She frequently thanked me for being there with her. "I worry about Joseph and Jesus," she said to me as we began to lay out the cheese, dried fruits, and bread before dinner one evening. Jesus was lying in his crib, playing with a rag ball. "I don't know what I would do without you here. I carry many things in my heart, Gertrude. I have been alone for a long time, but it's nice to know there is someone I can turn to with my cares."

"I feel the same, Mary, thank you for letting me come along with you. I don't know what I would have done if you hadn't," I replied. "I think I would have been turned out if I had stayed in Bethlehem. I have seen many widowed women living in the streets because the male relatives would not take them in. I didn't have anyone to turn to really. And you have become like family to me."

"We feel the same. Joseph and I both appreciate everything you do. We're blessed to have you with us. Thank you for being obedient to Eli when he told you to come find us," Mary said with tears of gratitude in her eyes.

"It was not something I have done easily, I must admit. Being obedient isn't always my first choice. Eli knew that very well. I suppose that is why he made me promise. He knew that trust has always been something sacred between us. Leaving was the hardest thing I have ever had to do. I have always wanted to do things my way, but there were times when I knew Eli was right, and I didn't rebel. When he asked to leave and find you, there was something in his voice, in his request, that spoke straight to my heart. I knew somehow I would do what he asked."

Mary's and Joseph's words were so nice to hear, but I truly felt like the lucky one, the blessed one, to be included in their lives. I couldn't believe how the time seemed to slip away in that quiet village. Soon Jesus was talking and walking around. He was a quiet and thoughtful child to be sure, but when he laughed, oh! It was something to behold. It was infectious and before long, we were all laughing without even knowing the cause.

As he began to talk, he couldn't pronounce my name and took to calling me Gee. I absolutely loved it. I had no children of my own, nor any nieces or nephews that I was close to, but I felt like an aunt to Jesus. He was so easy to love. I loved hearing, "Gee, you there?" as he would approach my door looking to see if I would play with him or go for a walk. No matter what I was doing, I always put it aside. I could never refuse him anything—a treat of dried fruit, raisin cake, or just simply my presence and undivided attention.

Jesus was so curious too. He wanted names for everything he could see and for so many concepts in his mind. I had been around children in my life, but none of them were like Jesus. He was not shy and liked playing with the other children. They were concerned with playing games and running around. Jesus typically could be found sitting under the olive trees, looking at the sky as though he was seeing something we could not. Sometimes I forgot how little he was when he would sit quietly next to my loom as I wove linens. He would wait until I took a break before bothering me with the next question on his mind.

We had many conversations about things I thought beyond his age of reason. He asked me how I prayed and to whom I prayed. When I told him I prayed to God, he said, "That's good, Gee, that's who you are supposed to pray to, for now." When I asked what he meant by "for now," he just shrugged his shoulders and said, "You'll see." It seemed to me that he knew the answer and chose not to reveal it.

When he looked at me during those talks, I felt his eyes look into my heart, and he knew me better than I knew myself. I was never ashamed to tell him anything about myself. How could this little boy be so wise?

As years went by and Jesus grew into adolescence, his wisdom was astonishing. Jesus excelled in his Scripture studies. He loved to tell us about the lessons and repeat from memory the scriptures he was learning. He was so natural when he spoke of the prophets I thought he knew them somehow. Of course that couldn't be, thinking it was just his enthusiasm.

One afternoon we were sitting under a large olive tree next to my cottage. I was telling him again the story of his birth on the occasion of his tenth birthday. I had repeated his birth story every year as my own mother did for both my brother and me. I always loved hearing her tell me how much she loved me the moment I was born. Hearing it affirmed how wanted and loved I was. She remembered every detail of it and never skipped a year of telling it, till her death.

Now, although I am not his mother, I wanted to honor her and carry on the same storytelling. Each year after his birthday meal, Mary and Joseph would listen quietly while I told Jesus the story of his parents' arrival in Bethlehem at our inn. They never added anything to my telling, nor did they ever contradict any detail. Jesus always waited for the story to begin. He would ask about Eli and about the baby boy, Caleb, that Eli tried to save. It seemed to get easier to talk about losing him after each telling. The pain lessened, but the memory remained clear and distinct in my mind.

Each year as I finished the story, we would share a long moment of silence. Then Jesus would usually break it with a question. One year, he asked, "Gee, Eli was so brave to go to your neighbors and try to save their boy. Where do you think he got that kind of courage?"

"I'm not sure, Jesus. He was a quiet, generous man and was never really known for great courage. I guess God must have inspired him to act in such a way."

"You are right, you know. It was the Father who gave Eli the courage to do what he did—even if it cost him his life.

There is no greater love than that—to lay down your life for another. And the reward for that is eternal happiness. Eli has been given that reward, Gee, I promise," he said with confidence beyond his years.

"Jesus, how do you know this and how can you make such a promise?" I questioned

"Gee, trust me, I know," he answered, moving close to me and put his arms around me, hugging me tight.

Through my tears, I welcomed his embrace and felt my trust in this boy soar.

9

When Herod had died,
behold, the angel of the Lord appeared in a dream
to Joseph in Egypt and said,
"Rise, take the child and his mother
and go to the land of Israel,
for those who sought the child's life are dead."
He rose, took the child and his mother
and went to the land of Israel…
and because he had been warned in a dream,
he departed for the region of Galilee.
He went and dwelt in a town called Nazareth,
so that what had been spoken through
the prophets might be fulfilled,
"He shall be called a Nazorean."

—Matthew 2:19–23 (NAB)

We lived peacefully for several years in Egypt. One day Joseph gathered us together before the morning meal. "We can go home now," he said with a smile.

"What? Are you sure?" Mary asked as she set dishes on the table.

"Yes. The angel of the Lord appeared to me again last night in another dream and said, 'Rise, take the child and his mother and go to the land of Israel, for those who sought the child's life are dead.'"[1]

Mary's hand went to her heart, and I sat dumbfounded. It was a mix of emotions for me. I had come to feel as though this village was home. I didn't want to go back to Bethlehem. Eli's family seemed foreign to me now. My parents and brother were long dead, leaving me with no living immediate family. I did have relatives in Cana but had not seen them for many years.

"Oh, Gee, isn't this wonderful news?" Mary said, calling me by the same name as Jesus did. She clasped my hand in hers, and I felt the warmth. "Can it be that King Herod has passed? I know I should not be overjoyed by the news of someone's death, but I do miss my family."

"But, Mary, we are to go to the town of Nazareth. This is what God has revealed to me. It will be a new beginning for all of us. I have only one project that needs finishing, and

---

[1]   Matthew 2:20 (NAB)

then we can leave I should be finished with it today, so you and Gee should start to gather our belongings." Joseph finished his breakfast, kissed his wife, and headed off to work.

Mary heard his words and remained quiet. I knew she had hoped to return to Nazareth, the hometown of her parents. I heard her begin to hum while we laid out the breakfast meal and she began assisting Jesus with his food.

"We should begin packing," Mary said after our meal was over.

"Yes," I said absently as I began to gather the dishes to wash, not sure of what to think.

Quietly, Mary stepped behind me and placed her hand on my shoulder. "You will come with us, won't you, Gee?"

Again, it was as though she could read my mind. Her first thought at Joseph's news had been joy at being reunited with her family. She was eager to introduce them to her son. But my first thought had been a fear of being separated from my new family. I worried that they wouldn't want or need me around anymore. Eli always needed me to help in the running of the inn. I found a lot of satisfaction in being needed by him and by our guests. Was this news the end of their need for my service?

I turned to her with tears in my eyes. Mary had been such a good friend to me, and I felt silly for doubting that friendship. Now both of us would be heading to a new town together. Jesus bolted from his chair and grabbed my hands.

Jesus chimed in and said, "Yes, Gee, you have to come. You can't leave me."

I laughed then. "Of course not, little one. I will never stray from your side."

"Then it's settled," Mary added.

So relieved by their invitation, I had tears welling up once again. Tears had never come easy for me. They had always seemed to be a sign of weakness. But since coming to live with Mary and her family, my tears had become too familiar. When I allowed them to flow, I always felt better. I realized the healing effect they had on me. I came to appreciate the gift my tears had for me and did not stifle them any longer.

On this day, tears of gratitude flowed easily. Mary came and put her arms around me, her own tears of love flowing as we stood in silence for a long moment. Jesus reached around both of us and squeezed us tightly. The three of us danced around in a circle—laughter and tears flowing from within.

We were embarking on yet another journey but this time were leaving together, as a family. I had never been happier in my life.

My mood lifted, I went about my tasks with a smile. That day we began our preparations to leave. We had some happy memories in this place, but it had never been the plan to stay here forever. Joseph's dream telling him to leave

Bethlehem was clear—they were to stay in Egypt until he was told to leave. And now in yet another dream, he was given the clear message that their time in Egypt was ended.

This time our departure was not hurried, which meant that we could make the proper arrangements. When we had arrived with our meager possessions from Bethlehem, we had to work hard and get by on little. Now, we would be able to use a cart and team and take our possessions with us. This journey would be much easier for all of us than when we had each left the inn that fateful night many years ago.

I knew that the things I had accumulated over the years running the inn didn't mean much, and it was heartening to know how well I had been able to get by without them. My leaving to find Mary, Joseph, and Jesus was more important than any material possession I had. But at the same time, I was now proud of my weaving and didn't want to have to start over on some of the pieces I had recently begun to work on. I would be able to take my supplies with me. Also, bowls, bedding, and even seeds for a new garden would be able to make this trip. It lightened my worries to know these things. Mary had become an accomplished weaver under my tutelage. We had enjoyed many hours of weaving, talking, and laughing.

Later that evening as I prayed, I asked God, *How is it I can feel so lonesome for my Eli and yet be excited about the future with this move? What a great price I've paid for this freedom to follow Mary and become part of her family.* I pondered this question for quite some time when at last I heard that familiar whisper.

It's not a price, my beloved Gee, but a reward to standing faithful and praying big, a lot and always.

I was greatly consoled by what the spirit revealed to me and quite joyful to hear him address me by the same abbreviated name Jesus had been using for me - Gee.

The journey to Nazareth was uneventful. We weren't fleeing an enemy, and I wasn't racing to catch up to them. It was a homecoming, and each one of us knew it. Even Jesus knew this was an exciting time and couldn't wait to meet the rest of his family. Mary couldn't wait to see her cousin Elizabeth. She was giggling and talking about her past like she was still a young maid. It was quite a sight to behold and endeared her all the more to my heart.

We settled into a small house in Nazareth of Galilee. Again, I stayed in a room in the rear of their house where I had room for my weaving and a warm bed to sleep in. Most of my time was spent out in the garden or in the main kitchen helping Mary.

A few days after our arrival home, we attended a gathering of the townsfolk after Sabbath. A huge party was thrown in Mary and Joseph's favor as their family members wanted to welcome them back. They had come from all over to see their long-lost kin.

They were all very open and warm to me as well. Mary's cousin Elizabeth in particular sought me out to thank me for helping with the delivering of Mary's baby. She placed her hand on my head and said a small blessing over me. It brought a smile to my face, and I felt like I was really a part of the family. Most of the visitors fawned over our little Jesus, who took it all in stride. Most children would have let all of that attention go to their heads and start to act out, but not our little man. He thanked everyone for their kind words and remained quiet and humble through it all.

There were a couple though who tried to put a damper on the party. An older couple sidled up to me as the day turned to evening. "He's a little strange, isn't he?" the woman asked with a crooked grin.

I was smiling as Jesus was being kind to the other children at the party. "Strange? In what way?"

"Well, he's so quiet and pensive. He doesn't run around like the other kids," she stated.

"I wouldn't call that strange," I said, feeling I was quickly going to lose my patience with this judgmental woman. "I think the word you mean is special. He's a very special boy, and soon enough everyone will know just how special he is."

"Well, he doesn't look much like Joseph," the woman said, glaring at Jesus intently.

I frowned at her. There was that gossip thing coming back. It occurred to me that not everybody at the party had good intentions. I had no patience for this unkind talk. "They're a beautiful family, and I'm happy to be a part of it. And may I say, ma'am, you have no idea what you are talking about. Joseph is his father, and there is no one here who can dispute that, least of all you," I said finally and turned away from her. I knew it was rude of me, but I didn't care.

The woman pursed her mouth shut, clearly biting back a retort. Her husband grabbed her elbow and steered away from me as I crossed my arms over my chest defiantly. I wasn't going to let them ruin this night, and I made it my duty to make sure they didn't get near to Mary. She didn't need to hear the rude comments and insinuations against her character. I would protect my friend and her son from any insult that they might accidently overhear.

The next few years seemed to slide easily by living in Nazareth. There were no dark clouds hanging over our heads. Joseph's skills as a carpenter were in high demand, and I had no trouble selling my linens at the market each week. I was even commissioned by a couple of city officials to make tapestries to hang in their halls. It was quite sobering to be so esteemed. Although it felt good to be recognized for my gift, I always strived to remain humble, knowing the source of it all.

As I finished each piece, I offered it to the Father, in thanksgiving for my skill and for all he had done for me. Many of my pieces depicted scenes from our sacred scriptures as I imagined them: Adam and Even in the lush Garden of Eden, Moses in his little basket being pulled from among the reeds, and Jonah as he was swallowed by the whale. Other pieces depicted beautiful landscapes that I'd seen from my travels, the busy city of Bethlehem, the vast desert of Egypt, and the little villages we encountered along the way.

Jesus was showing promise of taking after his father. He showed a fair amount of skill in woodworking and would often accompany Joseph to help with some of the easier tasks, but most of the time Jesus was still a child and curious about the world. He still wanted names for everything and seemed determined to learn as much as possible about the world.

One afternoon though, he came into the house distraught and carrying something small in his hands. "Mother, I need help," he said to Mary, who was busy washing some fabric. Her hands were wet up to the elbow.

"Come here, Jesus. Let me see if I can help you," I said so he wouldn't disturb Mary in the middle of her task. Mary nodded to the both of us in ascent as I set aside my embroidery and drew him near. "What do you have there?"

Jesus opened up his hands to reveal a small white bird. It barely moved as I observed it. "He's hurt, Gee, and I don't think he can fly. I want to help him," Jesus said with concern in this voice.

I took the little bird into my hands and felt along its tiny body. I saw that the feathers on one side of his body were all bent the wrong way. This was more than just a broken wing. This bird seemed to have some internal injuries that could not be helped. I pressed my fingers into the bird's side and could feel a bulge where there shouldn't be one. This bird was beyond any help we could provide. I looked into Jesus's eyes, and they looked beyond their twelve years.

"I'm sorry, my boy, but he's gravely injured. We can make him comfortable, but there's nothing else we can do for him. Why don't you get that basket in the corner and fill it with some nice clean straw, and I'll see if I can get him to drink some water."

He nodded and went out to the garden to gather supplies to make a nest for the bird. I tried to tempt the poor creature with some water, but it refused even a sip. I felt so bad for the animal but even more so for Jesus. This would be his first direct encounter with death, and I felt helpless to shield him from the ugly truth of life.

All evening, Jesus wouldn't leave that little bird's side, and only after a mild scolding from Mary, he went off to bed. I was worried that Jesus would wake in the morning to find that bird unresponsive in its little nest. I tossed and turned until I decided sleep wasn't for me that night. I didn't want to see my little Jesus upset for any reason. I decided to go check on the wounded bird.

The sky was clear and bright with a large full moon hanging overhead and lighting up the garden. I made my way to the bench Joseph had made for Mary and me. I stepped carefully, not wanting to disturb the night, but I gasped quietly when I saw a small figure sitting on the bench where the basket containing the bird had been left for the night.

"Jesus, what are you doing out here?" I asked as I sat down next to him.

"I couldn't sleep," he said. "I wanted to be out here with my bird."

"You should have told someone. You shouldn't be out at night alone, especially in the cold." I scooted closer to him and wrapped one side of my shawl around him. "How is your little charge doing?" I asked, afraid of the answer, wondering if the bird had died.

Jesus pointed to the bush in front of us, and I had to squint to see but perched on a limb sat the little white dove.

"It's a miracle!" I nearly shouted. "How on earth did he get there? I must have read his injuries wrong or you have become a very good healer," I said with a laugh. I watched in wonder as the bird sat contentedly on its branch and chirped quietly to us. It didn't seem scared to be near to us.

Jesus didn't say anything. He just smiled at me and leaned into my side. "Are you going to tell mother that I came out here?" he asked after a few moments of silence.

"You know I have no secrets from your mother," I said quietly. "Besides, she'll wonder what happened to the bird."

"Okay," he said. He wasn't pouting or upset. We both knew he wouldn't really get in trouble. We stayed there for quite a long while, watching the miracle bird sit on that branch.

When the first rays of the morning sun bathed the garden in light, we spotted the white dove perched on the same branch. It seemed to acknowledge Jesus, cooed, and then flew off.

Mary questioned me about the bird. When I told her what happened, she only smiled and continued with her chores, storing this too in her heart.

Every year, the whole family traveled to Jerusalem to celebrate Passover. We usually stayed with relatives for a few days and followed all of the customs of the festival. It was always a happy time of year but also a time for us to reflect on the promises of God. It was a great reminder to me to know that God actively watches over his people. I knew in my heart that he stands faithful and loves us even when we do not return that love.

I remained devoted to my prayers and journaling through the years. Mary and I had become accustomed to praying every morning before we started the day's chores. We wouldn't even set a pot to boil until the last "Amen." Each day, I was amazed at the blessings that were showered on me. I still couldn't believe my luck for having been welcomed into this family so fully. Not only had God given me a friend in Mary who was always willing to listen and share my pain, it seemed she never tired of hearing the stories I loved telling about the people Eli and I met while running the inn. She never judged me, especially when I recounted times when my impatience got the best of me. She loved me like a sister and like a mother all at once.

Usually our talks ended up including Jesus. When I spoke about being frustrated with a rude customer at the inn, she would remind me that since I had come to live with them, those traits had all but disappeared. She believed that my love for Jesus had replaced any anger I previously held onto. She told me that it was probably why the Father led me out of Bethlehem, even though tragic circumstances were the cause of my leaving.

Mary also told me one day after our morning prayer how proud of me she was. "You know, Gee, I love you very much. I really love how you pray. You are not afraid to bear yourself to the Father. I heard you ask him to show you the woman he sees when he looks at you. That takes courage to be willing to see yourself through his eyes. I think that's why your impatience and anger have been tamed so much. He has shown you this sin and has given you a reason to overcome it. Jesus is that reason, Gee. Thank you for loving my son. I prayed that you would that day he was born, and I offered him to you to hold. I believe we were destined to be together. I am grateful to God, our Father, and to you for accepting him into your heart."

As I listened to her words, I knew there was truth in them. I was humbled to learn how well she knew me and my struggles. I did pray that God would reveal to me how to be a woman of faith that he would be pleased with. I failed many times but felt his mercy and forgiveness. I knew now that my finding the love I felt for this woman and her child was from a divine source. I was being transformed by this love and wanted the change to be complete. I promised God that I would cooperate with the grace he gave me in order to accomplish what that little baby boy started in the stable.

When Jesus was twelve, we again made the trip to Jerusalem for the Jewish celebration of Passover. After the celebration, we all began the long journey home. Mary and I were walking among the women, while Joseph went up ahead, traveling with the men. When we stopped for the midday meal, I noticed that Jesus was not with Joseph as he came to join us. When questioned, he said that he assumed Jesus was with us. Jesus was missing. We checked with everyone in our caravan, and nobody had seen him. He had never done anything like this before, and all three of us became worried. "He must still be in Jerusalem," Joseph said. "I'll go back and find him."

"No," Mary said. "We'll all go help you look for him."

We turned back while the rest of the group continued on to Nazareth. We searched everywhere we had been over those three days. We checked in with friends and family, but nobody had seen any sign of Jesus. We were frantic with worry. After all we'd been through all these years, to lose him by accident was unthinkable. My impatience to find him was getting the best of me. Finally, we came up to the temple and entered. It was the last place we hadn't looked. If he wasn't there, we didn't know where to turn next. We would probably have to notify the city guard to help in our search for him. I knew there was no way Mary, Joseph, or I would leave Jerusalem without their precious boy.

As we reached the entrance of the temple, Joseph saw him first. There he was, sitting among the temple's teachers. They seemed to be engaged in a deep discussion as the three of us approached. Jesus listened closely while others spoke and then raised his own questions, which set them all to thinking. He was sitting as though he were an equal among them. Nobody doubted him for his age, and yet they marveled at his wisdom.

We walked up to him. It was Mary who spoke, "Son, why have you done this to us? Your father and I have been looking for you with great anxiety." I knew she was trying to hide her worry.

And he said, "Why were you looking for me? Did you not know that I must be in my Father's house?"[2]

Joseph and Mary led the way from the temple, and Jesus followed obediently. I trailed behind, afraid he might take off on his own again. "Why would you scare your parents like that?" I asked once we were outside of the city, and I knew Jesus would now be following his parents.

"Gee, I was about my Father's business," Jesus said without a hint of sarcasm.

"What do you mean? Your father was worried about you. He didn't send you to the temple for anything. He surely would never have left you there."

"I did not mean to worry anybody, but I was sent to the temple with a purpose," he said.

I opened my mouth to scold him but was quickly quieted. Jesus looked me in the eyes, and not for the first time, I saw more there than a twelve-year-old boy. I was reminded

---

2   Luke 2:46–49 (NAB)

of years ago when I looked into his eyes for the first time after his birth when I vowed to love this boy. Deep in those eyes was understanding beyond measure. He knew more of this world than I could ever hope to understand, and I knew he had a purpose beyond being loved by me. I just didn't know then what it truly meant.

We traveled the rest of the way home without further incident. No one mentioned what happened again. It seemed to me that an air of seriousness settled over our family after that trip. We all knew something had changed with Jesus. I thought about his remark "my Father's business" and pondered his meaning.

I was still wrestling with the idea of Jesus being the Savior I had prayed for so long ago. God still hadn't given me a clear answer to my question. I worried that maybe God was angry with me for some reason. I was doing my best, but maybe it wasn't good enough. It just seemed unfathomable that this boy whom I loved so much could be the answer to the world's problems. His remark in the temple was the first time I'd heard it said out loud. I supposed that it was a striking reality for Mary and Joseph as well. What did it mean to them? It surely never changed how they doted on him and raised him to be an upright young man.

10

◄ ———————— ►

And he said to them, "Why were you looking for me?
Did you not know that I must be
in my Father's house?"
But they did not understand what he said to them.
He went down with them and came to Nazareth
and was obedient to them,
and his mother kept all these things in her heart.
And Jesus advanced in wisdom
and age and favor before God and man.

—Luke 2: 49–52 (NAB)

AFTER OUR RETURN from Jerusalem, I began to watch Jesus even more closely. Of course, I had watched him all of his life, but before, I just marveled at every little thing he accomplished. Now I knew there was so much more to him being special. As he grew older, he spent less and less time with his peers and other children. He would often disappear for an hour at a time always with the same pensive look.

One day while Mary was gone to the market and Joseph was at work, I let my curiosity get the better of me. Jesus had again gone off on his own, and I couldn't help but follow him. I knew it was wrong of me to invade his privacy, but I followed anyway.

He was heading away from town when I saw him up ahead. He knew I was behind him because he slowed his pace enough that I easily caught up to him. We didn't talk for some time, and I realized then that Jesus was about to surpass me in height. *Where had the time gone?* I wondered.

"How do you know about the world, Gee?" Jesus asked me to break the silence.

It was such a thought-provoking question that I had to take a moment to come up with an answer. Some adults might have laughed at Jesus for asking something so odd, but I knew that he had given it some serious thought and wanted a real answer. "Well, I guess my parents taught me most of the things I know. I've observed a lot as well. I never had any real schooling, but my father taught me how to read and write. Eli taught me how to keep books when we ran the inn," I said. "I've been around for a while. I guess I've learned from the life experiences I've had.

"And what about your weaving? Did somebody teach you how to do that?"

"Yes and no," I said. "My mother taught me how to sew and weave fabric. She even taught me the basics of embroidery, but her designs were simple and not too complicated. I have come to love the more intricate designs. Mind you, I'm not saying this to brag, but much of what I can do with thread and fabrics comes from my fingers somehow. I know that God is the true source for my ability to weave and ply thread. I love him for blessing me with such a passion for needlework." I spread my hands out in front of me and extend them toward Jesus. "Does that make any sense?"

"Yes, Gee, it makes a lot of sense, and it is your truth," he said, holding my hands. We stopped on the path we were walking as he examined my hands and turned them over to look at my palms. He looked closely at the wrinkles, knuckles; then, he lifted my hands and kissed them softly.

We resumed our walk in silence. I could tell there was so much more on his mind, but I didn't want to press him. I just let him work out things in his head and knew that he would ask another question when he was ready to talk again.

"I think I am the same," he said. He stopped in his tracks and looked at me. "I know what I've learned from my parents. And from you, Gee," he said with a chuckle. "But I feel like I know so much more than that. I know why the animals do what they do and why people act a certain way. I know the many promises from God. I feel I know God's heart, and I need to share it with others. This is what God has called me to do. I am becoming more aware of my true destiny every day. I am anxious for it to begin. I know my parents are my parents, but I have a deep growing knowledge of my Father. I don't mean Joseph. I mean my true Father. He is the same Father you pray to, Gee. I'm not sure where he ends and I begin. I feel as though I am he and he is me. Does that make sense?"

I suddenly felt breathless for some reason, as though I had just sprinted uphill. It made me dizzy but in a good way as though I was presented with a revelation. "We all strive to understand the heart of God and what he wants of us. I feel as though God called on me to help your family. There is no greater way for me to glorify God than to help your mother and father in raising you and put myself in service to them."

"Gee, you are a good daughter, and God is pleased with you. My father is pleased with you. I am pleased that you were obedient to him and followed after us. I am glad you are here with me today. I am pleased to be in your presence. I know how much you love me, Gee. And I love you big, a lot, and always. Don't ever forget that."

"Jesus, how can you know that God is pleased with me? I have so many faults. You know my impatience, my quick tongue." I felt breathless.

"I just know what God knows. He knows your heart and so do I. We like what we see there," he replied simply and with confidence.

My heart grew light as I stood in front of this boy who was almost a man. I could feel the transition starting to take hold. I could sense a day might come when I would have to testify to the world my love for him, and I hoped that I would be brave enough to stand faithful to that conviction.

We stood in silence for some time before Jesus took my hand and brought it up to his heart. I could hear the *thump, thump* of its beating and the warmth of his body. "I love you," he said.

"Oh and how I love you, my Jesus, my friend. You have been my joy all these years, especially since losing Eli back in Bethlehem. My heart was broken over his death. You helped me to see hope for the future. You brightened my darkest days." Tears pricked my eyes, and I had to swallow the sobs down. I felt again how special this boy was and, in particular, how special he was to God. I didn't know where this would take him, and for the second time in his life, I felt an unknown fear for him. I worried he was too special for this world.

Jesus came close and brushed a strand of my hair, "Gee, I'm sorry for your loss. You know sometimes God must remove an obstacle from your life in order for you to fulfill your true purpose. I know you loved Eli and your life at the inn. But coming with us is for a higher purpose. My mother needed your help in those early days of our exodus to Egypt. I believe you know this truth deep in your heart. God is truly pleased that you followed his prompting, made through Eli, to come and find us."

"Oh Jesus, you are so right. I've known for some time now that I belong with you and Mary and Joseph. This is where I want to be more than anywhere else. I would not change anything of the past. You know I prayed for a long time to find a friend like your mother. I am so grateful that Joseph brought her to our inn."

"Gee, you pray big. I know that God cannot resist you when you ask him with all your heart the way you do," Jesus replied as we continued our walk.

Jesus and I shared a special bond after that day. I had never kept anything from Mary, but I did keep our talk that day to myself. I treasured it in my heart beyond all else. But soon, I would have yet another secret to keep. I woke one morning with a horrible rash. It ran from my left side, all the way across my stomach. It was the worst pain I had ever felt in my life, and it came upon me suddenly. It flared red with painful bumps that turned into blisters by the end of the next day. Every little movement caused tears to well up in my eyes. Even the mere touch of the softest fabric was painful.

I could hardly move for days, and nothing Mary tried would make it go away. She tried giving me different remedies for pain, but they barely dulled the aches. Then she tried to apply different salves to the affected area, but they did no good. The pain eventually brought about a fever as some of the areas became infected. I was confined to my bed and could only take in water as I sweated in pain.

I lay as still as possible, sure that this would be the death of me. I focused all of my efforts into my prayers. There was only one person who could ease my suffering, and that was God. I gave up my pain and my life to God. I offered him everything in my prayers. I whispered aloud, "Lord, help me. Ease my suffering enough that I might say good-bye to those I hold most dear. I know everything is in your hands, but I cannot carry this burden without your help. It is too much for me. Nothing works to ease the pain, so, Lord God, I offer my pain to you. I beg of you to show mercy and to welcome me into your loving arms so I may see my Eli again. Amen."

I fell into a fitful sleep. In the middle of the night, I woke when I felt a slight touch on my side. It was gentle but startled me anyway. I expected to see Mary at my side, but instead, Jesus stood over me. He knelt at my bed and put his finger to his lips to encourage me to be quiet, then closed his eyes. He gently placed both hands on the most painful parts of my rash. I nearly cried out from the pain.

But then something miraculous happened. The pain began to ease, little by little, until there was no pain at all. I thought maybe Jesus had found a salve to help with the pain and heal the wounds of the rash. Before long, I could move without feeling the stab of daggers in my side. I sat up in bed and felt as good as ever. My fever had broken, and I could feel strength coming back into my body. I pulled the sheet back and saw that the rash had disappeared entirely. I felt on my stomach, and it was gone from there as well. I couldn't believe it.

"What?" I started to ask, but again, Jesus held his finger to his lips.

"I love you, Gee. God heard your prayers and sent me," he whispered as he slowly stood up and quietly walked out of the cottage and made his way back into the house. God had answered my prayers.

What really amazed me was Mary's reaction to my overnight cure. She came in to check on me the next morning and saw my skin had been healed.

"He came to you last night, didn't he? I knew he would hear you, Gee. He loves you more than you can imagine," she said and helped me to wash.

"Yes, Mary, he did. How did he know to come and what to do? How did he do this? And why did he do this?" I was still trying to make sense of it all.

"Because he knows the mind of God better than we can ever know. He knows what we need as God reveals it to him. Gee, don't you see, he and God, his father, are of the same mind," she replied.

Not long after my miraculous recovery, Joseph fell ill. His sickness was not a rash but a an illness which caused him to start coughing uncontrollably. He dismissed it initially and tried to continue his woodworking projects as usual, but Mary and I could both see his health starting to fail. Each morning, he seemed to be a bit slower to get up and start moving.

"Why don't you take a day off today?" Mary asked. "You work so hard, and you need some rest. Let me make you some soup. It will help your cough."

I also wanted to help and went right away to the market for some salve for Joseph. Its menthol effect would be soothing for cough. I gave it to Mary to apply to Joseph's chest. After giving in and staying home for the morning, Joseph seemed better. However, by midafternoon, he could not be held down.

"I have a project I need to finish. They're counting on me," Joseph said matter-of-factly before leaving the house.

"I honestly don't know what to do with him. He won't see that he's very sick," Mary said sadly.

"My Eli would never admit that he was sick either. He didn't want anyone to think he was weak, but in the end, he would end up laid up for days on end with a severe illness because he wouldn't take any remedy." I shook my head. "Some men are just like that."

"Maybe we should say a prayer for him," Mary suggested.

"Oh yes, let's pray now."

I knelt on the floor, and Mary knelt beside me. We bowed heads and held hands as Mary lifted her husband up to God to watch over him. I was reminded of the prayers I used to say over Eli's health. After a long prayer of intercession on Joseph's behalf, we both went back to our daily routines and waited for Joseph to arrive home.

It was apparent when he walked through the door that evening that he was not feeling well at all. His cough had gotten worse in the hours he was gone. His pallor was an ashy gray, and the cough racked his body visibly. He could barely stand long enough to wash the grime from his hands and face before he fell into a chair at the table.

Mary put her hand to his forehead. "My goodness, you have such a fever. You need to lie down. I'll bring your supper. Jesus, please help your father to bed."

The boy helped lift his father up, and I could see that Joseph was leaning heavily on his son's shoulders. I started chattering to fill the silence and ease Mary's worries. I wanted to pretend like Joseph's illness wasn't serious, but we could all tell that this was more than a cold. The next morning, Joseph didn't even try to get out of bed. I began the preparations for the morning meal, started the laundry, and kept up with the dishes so that Mary could focus on her husband. Joseph could barely tolerate even a little of the soup Mary had prepared for him. Each morning, we knelt on the hard floor together and prayed to God to restore Joseph's health, but each night, he went to bed in worse condition.

Jesus stayed close around the house during those days. Normally, he would go and help Joseph at work or wander on his own, but these days he remained very close to Joseph's side. He helped me hang the clothes on the line outside to dry in the sun. Then he helped me with our evening meal. We both wanted to make sure Mary could focus all of her attention on Joseph.

Finally, one day Mary was trying to coax Joseph to take even a spoonful of soup. Joseph was eating less and less each day and slept very little due to the coughing spells. The last several days had been difficult for Mary as she watched her husband grow weaker. I noticed blood in the coughing cloth Joseph used.

As Jesus was helping put the dishes away, I whispered to him, "Why can't you heal him? You helped me. Don't you see how worried your mother is?" I was feeling desperate. I knew what Jesus did for me and my rash. I thought of all people, Joseph deserved to be healed. Surely he was more favored by God than I.

Jesus looked at me quietly and gently put a bowl on a shelf. "Only the Lord can call his children home and only he knows the time for it. Gee, you still have work to do."

"But Joseph does too. He's still young," I began to plead.

Nothing else was said, and I knew that Joseph was, in fact, in God's care. It was difficult for me to think about that. Death had yet to really touch this little family, and I couldn't believe it would come to Joseph. That night, I pleaded with God and asked him why he would save me only to take Joseph. Why was my future important? I couldn't understand this reasoning. I offered my life in exchange for Joseph. I knew how much he loved his son and how much Mary relied on him. I would be happy to let this family stay together for as long as God allowed.

Before the sun had risen, I realized my prayers had not been answered. I didn't know what exactly woke me because my cottage and the garden were both silent. I put on a shawl and stepped outside. Across the courtyard, I could see the tiny flicker of candlelight in a window. In spite of it being so quiet and peaceful, I couldn't understand why my nerves were wound so tightly. I walked over to the main house and entered. I moved down the hallway toward Joseph and Mary's room. The door was ajar, and Mary kneeled over the side of the bed while Jesus stood behind her with his hands on her shoulders.

"What has happened?" I asked, fearing the worst.

"He has gone on to be with our heavenly father," Jesus said quietly.

Mary cried quietly and gently stroked Joseph's still hand. I fell to my knees beside her and wrapped my arm around her. I could feel her sobs shaking her entire body. We stayed in that tableau for a long time, and as the minutes ticked by, Mary began to transfer more and more of her weight into me. Before long, I had her wrapped entirely in my arms as she leaned on me. It was a moment when I accepted Mary's grief as my own. I cried with her. I stroked her hair as I prayed silently for God to minister to her broken heart. *Show her your mercy, Father. Give her courage to face her future without her husband, just like you did for me. She deserves it so much more than I.* After a long while, I felt her straighten up.

"Oh, Gee, I am so glad you are with me and Jesus. We can do what we must as long as we are together," Mary said as she wiped her eyes.

Jesus had left the room, and I could hear him in the kitchen. He came back and helped me lead Mary to the dining room table where he had cups of hot tea waiting for us. We sipped in silence and seemed to be in a daze for the rest of the day. There were so many preparations to be made. I felt almost relieved when I remembered that I had been working on a nice piece of linen that would work well for Joseph's burial shroud. It wasn't much, but it was one less thing that Mary would have to worry about. I wanted to do as much as possible to help ease the pain and burden she was feeling.

The burial arrangements were all made by the end of the day, and some men had already taken Joseph's body to be prepared for burial. I took a moment to seek out Jesus, who was sitting in the garden under the warm sun. "How are you doing?" I asked, ready to offer my shoulder for him to cry on. But he turned to me with a smile on his face.

"I am well," he said.

"How can you be taking this so easily?" I wondered. "Why are you not tearing your robe or questioning God for taking Joseph?" I never thought him capable of questioning God, but I would not have faulted him for it either. I wasn't used to someone so young accepting death so easily. I surely had not when I lost my Eli.

"I know my father is happy right now. He is in the kingdom of God and basking in the glory of God. He has no more hurts or troubles. I know that my Father is pleased with him and has welcomed him home," Jesus explained.

"Thank you, son," Mary said as she moved in front of us. She had been listening to our conversation and knelt before Jesus. She took his hands in hers. "Thank you for easing my mind."

I too could feel the peace radiating from the young man next to me. My doubts and fears were being quieted. I don't know why I didn't consider the fact that Joseph was at peace with God. He was sitting with the Father right now. I had been too worried about my own pains and sorrows that I hadn't realized his suffering was over.

"Death is not the end," Jesus said. "I promise you that there will be a way for life eternal as soon as God's plan is completed."

"How can you know such a thing?" I questioned.

"All has not been revealed, but be comforted for now," Jesus replied softly and with authority.

And we were comforted. I carried that in my heart for years afterward. The pain of losing Joseph was lessened by this eternal hope even though the place Joseph had in our lives would always remain empty. The most important people in my life were leaving me: my father, my brother, my babies, my Eli, and now Joseph. I would stand faithful amid all these losses because I had a strong assurance that I would see them again one day in the kingdom of God. Jesus had said it, even promised it. And I believed him.

11

It happened in those days that
Jesus came from Nazareth
of Galilee and was baptized in the Jordan by John.
On coming up out of the water he saw
the heavens being torn open and the Spirit,
like a dove, descending upon him.
And a voice came from the heavens,
"You are my beloved Son; with you I am well pleased."

—Mark: 9–11 (NAB)

MONTHS PASSED AS we settled into our regular days. Joseph was still in our hearts. Each day the pain eased, and we began to think about all of the good times and what a good father, husband, and friend he had been. I counted myself lucky to have been a part of his life.

I wondered if Jesus would take up Joseph's craft and continue working as a carpenter, but I could tell his heart wasn't in it. As he had told me before, his calling in life was to spread the word of God. It made Jesus happy to know of how many people were believers and followed God's law, but it tortured his soul to hear when someone had died without knowing the truth or refusing to believe it. It kept him up at night to think of all the people who didn't know the love of God and were disobedient.

Jesus had started to take even longer walks. He would leave for the day walking to nearby towns. Sometimes he would be gone for a day or two. After a while, he began to return with friends; he called them his disciples. Some of these men had been fishermen. They were following him to hear him talk about the kingdom of God. He spoke with authority and wisdom and inspired many to follow him. Some told Mary that Jesus had asked them to follow him and become fishers of men. Because of his charisma and manner of speaking, they felt compelled to follow him.

Mary and I followed Joseph and his friends one day near the Jordan River when we heard that John, the son of Mary's cousin Elizabeth, was preaching and baptizing many people. He was preaching about the coming of the Messiah with such passion and fervor that crowds followed him everywhere. We approached the crowd and made our way closer; I thought it was to hear John's preaching, but then Jesus walked on ahead of us. I heard him ask to be baptized just as we caught up.

John tried to prevent him, saying, "I need to be baptized by you, and yet you are coming to me."

Jesus said to him in reply, "Allow it now, for thus it is fitting for us to fulfill all righteousness."

Jesus was completely submerged, and when his head broke the surface of the water, what a sight! The sunlight glinted off the water droplets in his hair and gave him a halo of light. Just as Jesus was brought up out of the water, the heavens opened for him, and we all saw a dove coming to him, just above his head. I distinctly heard God's voice.

"This is my beloved son, with whom I am well pleased."[1]

I knew at that moment that everything I had been told about the baby boy I helped to deliver in that stable so many years ago was the truth. Then a familiar voice within my own heart spoke to me and said, *Gertrude, this man is the savior to the world. Everyone will have their moment to accept him as their redeemer or to reject him. Those who reject my son, also reject me. He has been sent to earth for a purpose. Will you accept him as your lord and savior?*

He was not just special. He was surely our Messiah, my Messiah. My faith grew even greater, as did my love for him. Mary and I followed his example and were baptized with the next group. As I came out of the water, I felt a

---

1   Matthew 3:13–17

surge of energy run through me. It was like a strong wave had hit my heart. As it receded, I was left with a serenity that overwhelmed my soul. Tears mixed with the waters of my baptism washed over me. I experienced a renewal of my faith in Jesus whom I knew was my Messiah. I responded to the voice, "Oh, yes, Father, I accept Jesus as my Lord and Savior, now and for all the days of my life."

After his baptism, Jesus left us and went into the desert, and we didn't see him for forty days and forty nights. I was distraught, but Mary waited patiently, sure that he would return. We knew in our hearts that God was with him and protecting him, but we still missed his presence with us. Mary and I lifted him up in our prayers every day and every night. We prayed that God would minister to him and reveal his plan for Jesus's life.

Mary prayed, "Father in heaven, guard my son, your son. Strengthen him for all that is to come his way. Grant him wisdom to teach everyone how they are to follow him. Give him your courage to face the temptations that will surely come to distract him from his purpose. Send your angels to minister to him. If it be your will, Father God, allow Gee and I to walk with him on the journey ahead."

I was amazed at Mary's prayer. She referred to Jesus as his son as well as her own. Her prayer was so intimate, so passionate. It seemed to me that she knew something about what was to come to Jesus. And it was not all good. What did she know? I was so curious to know more but kept quiet. We continued praying in silence.

When he returned to us sun-burnt, hungry, and thirsty, I praised God that he kept this most precious man alive. Jesus recounted his time in the desert to us and how Satan tried to tempt him away from his true path not once but three times. He fasted during his time out there and did not waiver in his devotion. The angels had ministered to him, and he was renewed before returning to us. I remained silent as I saw evidence of Mary's answered prayers for her son, his son.

In the weeks after Jesus's return, times were tough for us. Money for food was scarce. I was thankful that my linens and garments were still in demand. I knew we wouldn't go hungry. Maybe this was what God had kept me around for. Maybe this was my calling in life to help provide for this family and be there for Mary and her son. It might not have seemed like enough for some people, but it was more than enough for me. My service to them gave me purpose and was all I needed to be content with my life. I wanted for nothing more.

A week or so after he returned, Jesus came to me. "Gee, you have a letter," Jesus said as he knocked on the open door of my cottage.

I was in the middle of a complicated pattern, so I took a minute to finish my run before I put the shuttle down and accepted the parchment from Jesus. "Oh, it's from my cousin in Cana," I said with joy. "Jedidiah is getting married and has invited me to attend."

"That sounds like a grand reunion for you," Jesus said with a smile.

I held the letter to my chest. "I haven't seen any of my relatives in many years." I had lived in Bethlehem for so long that I didn't think I would ever see them again and had become resigned to that. I sighed. "I don't suppose I'll be able to make it. There is much to do here, and I don't want to travel alone."

"It's not so far away," he answered. "Mother and I could go with you. I would enjoy meeting some of your family."

"Oh, Jesus, do you mean it? That would be wonderful!" I exclaimed and jumped up to hug him. "Let's go tell Mary right now so we can make preparations."

Mary was just as eager as I was to have something to celebrate. We had all been sad for some time and looked forward to happy tidings. She was also eager to meet some of my family. She knew so much about them because I had shared the details of my childhood and lineage with her after meeting her family years before. Sometimes I needed to remind myself that I did in fact have family out there who had been a big part of my life at one point.

Mary, Jesus, several of his disciples, and I all left early with plenty of time before the wedding. I wanted to have as much time with my family as I could. I was so thankful for the company of Mary and Jesus though. We rode in the cart together, and I said, "I don't know why, but I'm very nervous." I was wringing my hands together and wanted the cart to both hurry up and to slow down.

"Well, I can understand your feeling, Gee. You haven't seen them in so long. I was nervous when we came to Nazareth as well. I knew what people had been saying before we left, and I worried what they would say when we came back," Mary admitted. "But everything is in God's hands regardless. And I am here for you—for anything you need. I'm sure this will be a happy occasion for everyone."

"Oh, I know you're right, Mary. Thank you for coming. It means everything to me to be able to share this happy time with you. You are so dear to me. I hope you know how much I love you." I held her hand, and her steadfastness helped to calm my nerves. By the time we reached Cana and the place of the wedding was within sight, I felt steady again. Mary always knew how to calm and reassure me that all would be well.

We arrived to a warm welcome. I introduced Mary, Jesus, and his friends who had also accompanied us to the celebration of my relatives. No one questioned us about how we all came to be together. After I told them of my two children and Eli's untimely death, I received condolences and offers of a place to live if I decided to stay on in Cana after the wedding. I was grateful for their kindness and generosity, but I know where I belonged. Mary and Jesus were my family now.

There was such a hustle and bustle going on when we arrived. The preparations were well underway, and every time I offered my assistance, I was told to just relax. I laughed every time and said, "If you knew me well, you'd know I have a hard time with that."

Finally, my cousin said with a smile, "There's no better time to practice than now, Gertrude. Please, just enjoy your time and reacquaint yourself with the family. We have all missed you." He hugged me and then flew off to help with the preparations.

He was right. I needed to just enjoy reuniting with my relatives. I introduced Mary and Jesus to everyone. There were some relatives whom I had not seen since we were children, and now they had families of their own. There were a few family members that I kept looking for, only to find out that they had joined God in the kingdom of heaven. But there were so many new people to meet: new spouses, children, grandchildren, cousins, aunts, and uncles. My own parents had passed on so many years ago, but it was great to hear stories of them. Some people even had stories of me running around, getting into trouble, and bossing the other kids around. That definitely sounded like me and made Mary and Jesus laugh in agreement. They delighted in hearing about my childhood. I sat, not in humiliation but rather with a sense of humility, at hearing the truth of myself. I could see how much I had changed during the years I'd lived with my new family, and I loved the new person I was becoming.

There was a group of young men there that Jesus instantly took a liking to. They began to discuss the word of God and theology so deeply that I again marveled at his knowledge. He truly seemed to be in his element there.

Mary was a delight to everyone. They eagerly asked questions about what we had been up to all these years. Mary rained praise on me that caused me to blush in embarrassment. She made me sound like a much better person than I was. I realized what a true friend she was to me.

The ceremony was beautiful. It reminded me that I hadn't attended a wedding since my own. Tears flowed as I realized the love that this couple would come to know. All of the emotions I had been feeling for so long all came to the surface in that moment. The tears were for so many reasons: my loss of Eli that I barely had time to mourn, the loss of my children that I would never see marry, the loss of Joseph so recently, but also the joy of having a friend like Mary, the pride I felt in watching Jesus interact with others, and the knowledge of God's love within my own heart. Mary came up next to me, put a gentle arm around my shoulder, and patted my hand while I wiped the tears away with a white linen handkerchief she had given to me before our journey to Cana.

After the vows, it was time for the wedding meal, and my cousin hadn't held anything back. There was so much food that I wondered how on earth it would all be eaten, but the wedding had been a big affair, and there were a large number of villagers. Many of the foods I had never heard of or seen before were served, so it was a real treat for all of us to experience this feast. I had become accustomed to the simple diet of bread, dried fruit, and nuts with occasional meat as we could afford.

After several hours into the party, my cousin walked by, and I stopped him to congratulate him, but he looked worried. "Cousin, is there something wrong? Can I help with anything?" I asked.

He looked side to side and then leaned in close to whisper, "We're almost out of wine. I don't know what I'm going to do. I thought I had calculated enough, but there isn't. We have run out of wine."

"Oh, dear," I said. "Let me see what I can do."

He looked at me puzzled when I said this; though I honestly didn't know what I could do about his problem. I sought out Mary to see if she knew how I could get out of this mess I just created for myself—offering to help when obviously I could not. I asked her what we could do to help out. "Maybe we could find a merchant and buy some wine. I do have some of my weaving money with me."

"Calm down, Gee," she said with a knowing smile. "Let's go to Jesus."

We found him and his disciples with the group of young men from before the ceremony. Jesus was at the center of the group, and I was reminded of when we found him in the temple of Jerusalem conversing with the teachers. Then he had been counted as an equal among those scholars; here he seemed to be the one they all looked to.

"Mother, what is it?" he asked when we approached the group. The men stepped aside and made room for us.

"They have no wine" was all she said to him.

Jesus said to her, "Woman, how does your concern affect me? My hour has not yet come."

Mary turned toward the servers and said, "Do whatever he tells you." She and I stepped to the side.

There were six stone water jars there for Jewish ceremonial washings, each holding twenty to thirty gallons. Jesus told them, "Fill the jars with water." So they filled them to the brim. Then he told them, "Draw some out now and take it to the headwaiter." So they took it.

And when the headwaiter tasted the water that had become wine, without knowing where it came from, although the servers who had drawn the water knew, the headwaiter went to my cousin and said to him, "Everyone serves good wine first, and then when people have drunk freely, an inferior one; but you have kept the good wine until now."[2]

I couldn't believe my ears or my eyes. Jesus had turned plain water into wine right before us all. I filled a cup for myself and tasted it. It was sweet and tasted better than any of the finest wine I had ever had. When I looked back to Jesus, he was surrounded by the men again who were in even more awe than I was. I had witnessed his miracles before, but they had been our secrets. This was a miracle for everyone to see and believe. I wondered, *Was this the beginning of the destiny Jesus had told me about years before?*

I looked over to Mary, and she was smiling at her son. I could tell she knew he was capable of a task like this, though she would have never said it. It wasn't in her nature to brag on her son's specialness. I wanted to shout it to the world right in that moment, but I took Mary's lead and only watched in wonder as the little boy I loved so much was being transformed into a man.

This became more apparent when Jesus decided to stay back an extra day when Mary and I headed home. He was so engaged with his conversations, and I couldn't fault him for clinging to this companionship. He had spent so much

---

[2] John 2:3–10

of his childhood alone or with only Mary and me for companionship. A young man needed to be among his peers and to learn about the world. Now, he was in his element, and he found other young men who were passionate about the teachings of God as well. They all came from such diverse backgrounds.

On the way home from the wedding, Mary could tell the change in her son as well, probably better than I. I felt proud and confident in his upbringing and knew that he would set a good example, but Mary looked worried.

"What's the matter?" I asked. "I know it must be hard to see Jesus go off on his own, but he's becoming a man, and you raised him well. He's a good boy, and you should be proud of him."

"Oh, Gee, I am very proud of him. He is truly his father's son and must follow his father's will. His journey will take him from us. I know he will stand faithful to it. I will miss him just as any mother would. We raise our children to be strong, to make wise decisions, and then to take their place in the world and be productive. Jesus's place in the world will save it. I am certain that things are about to change," she said. "Jesus is going to leave us soon."

"Leave us? Well, I suppose he does need friends of his own age and sort, but I don't see why he should need to leave us. You must be mistaken. He could never really leave us." I said the words, but I didn't really believe them. I hoped that maybe the more I said it wasn't true that it would be so.

"Gee, I know this to be true. Deep in my heart, I've always known that he would leave me and not like a young man leaves home to start a family. No, this is different. He's destined to be King, and now his journey toward that destiny has begun."

"King? He's going to be King? I thought he was our Messiah, not a King?" I replied.

"Do you remember what those wise men said the night Jesus was born all those years ago?"

I nodded. That night was permanently etched in my memory. I would never forget a single moment of it for the rest of my life. It set into motion all of the actions I have taken since that time.

"They came in search of a King, and they found Jesus. They found my son."

We fell quiet as the gravity of Mary's words hit me. King. Like the pieces of a puzzle, her words were starting to fit together in my mind with all of the events that had happened so far. I knew she didn't mean an earthly king, one who ruled over men and trivial pursuits of money and land. He wouldn't wage war on a perceived enemy. His battles would be much greater because we all had a common enemy that needed to be destroyed. His kingdom would be far greater than that of any man who had ever lived or would ever live.

Her words got me to thinking, *My Jesus, my friend would save the world? Save me?* I turned to the one thing I knew could help to clarify these things. "Let's pray," I said. There was really nothing else to do. Our prayers would do better work than our words. We needed God's help to get us through the difficult times to come but also to help Jesus. He would be in more need of our biggest prayers as he left the only home he's ever known to go out into the world and fulfill his calling.

We prayed during the rest of the journey home, sometimes silently and sometimes out loud and together. I even took to singing a couple of my favorite Jewish hymns. We were both quiet as we arrived home. We ate a simple dinner and went to bed early. We were both exhausted. Truthfully, I wanted some time to be alone with God.

I pulled out my prayer journal and began to flip through the pages. It contained many prayers from Jesus's years growing up. I found a prayer I had written down when Jesus fell ill with a fever. The poor boy was so distraught to be causing such a fuss in the household. He bore his pain in silence.

I flipped a few more pages and found a prayer I had written down asking God for forgiveness. I had let my tongue get the better of me and said things I had come to regret to a neighbor whose chickens got loose in our garden. Looking back, it was such a trivial moment, but I had let my anger take over. I went and apologized the next day. The neighbor forgave me and offered me a dozen eggs in return for the trouble. I was truly blessed and marveled at the mercy God showed me through my neighbor.

I wrote down my prayers that night again. I prayed for strength for all of us. I wanted to be there for Mary in this difficult time, but I also knew that I would need strength for myself as well. It would be hard to say good-bye to the boy I loved so much. I also prayed for guidance. Jesus was sure of his calling, but I was beginning to doubt mine now that he was leaving the household. I hoped my call to live with this family would not end with Jesus's departure and that Mary and I could continue to be together. I prayed that God would show me at least a small glimpse of where my path might lead me and how I could be of service.

I also prayed for peace. I could get myself wound up sometimes with all of my worries and excitement. I wasn't getting any younger. I prayed for peace to be able to look at each situation carefully and not run headlong into something I didn't fully understand. I wanted to follow God's guidance as best as I could but often found myself chasing after my own desires instead. I vowed yet again to be diligent in obedience.

The next day was another quiet day. Mary and I were sitting at the dining table when Jesus finally came home. *How could he have changed so much in a short time?* I wondered. I knew him so well and could see the conflicting emotions on his face. He smiled gently at us at the table, and I knew he was happy to know his mother had not been alone. That made me sit a little straighter in my chair, knowing that I truly was an integral part of this family.

"Won't you sit down, son?" Mary asked.

Jesus took the empty seat and looked at both of us. "I think you know what I'm about to tell you." We nodded, and he went on. "Mother, it is time. I must go to fulfill what my father has set in motion. It all began with you, my mother. You said yes to the Father, and I continue saying yes to him as well. I love you very much, Mother. You have been so good to me, teaching me the way I must go."

I nodded, tears welling up, as I listened to the exchange.

Mary looked distraught as Jesus kissed her and hugged her for a long moment. "I must go. My disciples are waiting." Jesus came to me, kissed me on the forehead, and said, "Gee, I thank you for being here with my mother. I love you for loving her. This is how it was to be. She invited you to love me at my birth and you accepted. I am well pleased, my beloved daughter. Remember when you pray, pray to the Father who sent me. You know this about me because my mother and Joseph have told you. You've known it with your head. But today, my dear sweet Gee, I want you to know me and my father with your heart. The truth is that my father sent me to save you. We both know your struggles—your impatience, you losses, and all your sins. My father asked me to come and save you, Gee, my daughter. I saw you, I loved you, and I said *yes* to the Father. I will make the way that you might enjoy my father's company. The price will be great, but know that I love you enough to pay it for you. Will you help me teach others who do not know I am sent by my Father that I am the only way to him? Keep praying as big as you always have. I wish everyone prayed as big as you. Tell others how you pray. Tell them about writing their prayers. It will help them."

I was confused by his words. He had certainly never called me daughter, and yet it seemed like a familiar truth to me. "I will, Jesus, I will. I will never forget what you have done for me. You taught me how to be at peace with myself and how to love others even when they bother me so. I am grateful that I have had the chance to come to know you and love you." I let the tears flow without control.

As Jesus walked out of the house, I could see that Mary was crying too. She seemed to be in such pain. My heart was moved with such love and compassion for her I thought I was not capable of. I touched her arm, and together we knelt to pray. I knew that she would be saddened and troubled to receive word of his travels and what would become of him. The dishes could wait, the gardening could wait, and even my weaving could wait. A talk with God could not wait.

I prayed aloud, "Lord, Father, help Jesus to be strong in fulfilling your plan. You know our hearts and the pain we feel at seeing Jesus leave us. We want to follow him, and yet this is our home. Help us to know your will. Please release us from this home and show us clearly if we should join Jesus and travel with him and the others." Mary squeezed my hands tightly as I continued, "We would be honored to be a witness to the works and teachings of your son. It would be a privilege to share your word as well. We wish only to glorify your name and praise you. We wish to bring nonbelievers into the fold and help them to know that Jesus is the way. Father, give us a sign of your desires. Amen. Oh, and I want to show others how to pray big—the way you taught me. Jesus said I should do this."

I opened my eyes and looked at Mary. I felt peace and clarity wash over me. It was as though I had lived my whole life with a film over my eyes, clouding my sight to the true brilliance of life. Now that film had been washed away, and I could see everything clearer than ever before. I was certain that we were to leave our home and follow Jesus.

Mary looked at me and nodded solemnly. "Yes, Gee, we are to go," she said as though she already knew that we would leave. This was God's way of showing us the path to take, and we eagerly accepted the challenge. For it would truly be a challenge to leave all we had ever known to venture on this journey. But we were ready and, more importantly, willing.

12

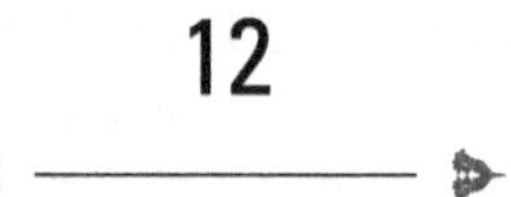

—Matthew 4:23 (NAB)

I WAS FILLED with anticipation to get started. Jesus was leaving, and we wanted to leave with him. Our lives changed dramatically with that discernment in our spirits and decision to follow along with Jesus. Mary and I walked through our home one last time. My little cottage had become very comfortable, with plenty of room for my loom and weaving supplies. I knew now that I could easily leave everything behind if it meant I could follow my Jesus. These material things were nothing in comparison to what Jesus had for me. I realized how detached I had become to my possessions, many things that we might have clung to otherwise.

I knew I had a gift with my weaving, but now I was able to see the bigger picture, and it just didn't make sense to lug around a large loom. Besides, I didn't have as much time to work on my craft anymore. I had more important roles to fill. In a way, I would be back to my days as an innkeeper's wife. There would be cooking and cleaning up after an interchanging group of people as Mary and I followed Jesus and his disciples.

We did not just stand as witness to the works of Jesus. We prepared meals for the men and any other travelers who wished to break bread with us. We gladly washed clothes after long days of traveling came to an end. I was able to put my sewing skills to use when I mended garments and helped to create new ones. It was actually a great way for us to minister as well. While down by the river washing clothes, we came into contact with many women who otherwise might not hear the word of God. Mary and I would strike up conversations with these women and their children and praise the blessings that God had rained upon us.

There was no greater feeling in the world than leading someone to God. We encouraged them to seek out Jesus as well, as he preached the word. We always knew where he would be, and many of those women encouraged their husbands to go listen as well. I passed on some of my own skills as a wife, teaching the women different ways to broach a subject with their husbands. I knew that not all men were like Eli, who freely accepted and embraced their wife's opinions. But I knew there were ways for a wife to suggest an idea to her husband with respect and love. I'd learned these lessons the hard way and was happy to share my wisdom. Marriage can be difficult if respect is not given or received. I spoke to the women about my marriage to Eli in hopes that they would learn from my mistakes. All of our efforts were only for the glory of God and to grow the ministry of Jesus.

It amazed me each day that we were able to get by. At night when we would go to bed and the food was running low, Mary and I prayed about how we would get through the next day. We asked God to show us a way to continue to feed and take care of his workers, and each day we never wanted for anything. There was always a way to get what we needed. God provided for his followers. I never ceased to be amazed at his providence to those of us who stood faithful to his word.

A truly spectacular sight was watching Jesus perform miracles and preach to the masses. He went all over Galilee, curing those who were sick and casting away demons. His fame began to spread so much that people as far as Syria were bringing their sick loved ones to be cured at his hands. Crowds began to follow Jesus around, and one day he decided to go up a mountain. The crowd followed to hear him speak.

Blessed are the poor in spirit,
for theirs is the kingdom of heaven.
Blessed are they who mourn,
for they will be comforted.
Blessed are the meek,
for they will inherit the land.
Blessed are they who hunger and thirst for
righteousness,
for they will be satisfied.
Blessed are the merciful,
for they will be shown mercy.
Blessed are the clean of heart,
for they will see God.
Blessed are the peacemakers,
for they will be called children of God.
Blessed are they who are persecuted for the sake of
righteousness,
for theirs is the kingdom of heaven.[1]

These words touched the hearts of everyone who heard them with an open mind to hear the truth. I was particularly moved by Jesus's words. There was a place in my heart that would always be in mourning. Now, hearing Jesus talk of the comfort I would one day receive gave me a renewed

---

[1]   Matthew 5:3–10 (The Beatitudes)

hope that I would surely see Eli and my babies again. His words also taught me of the kind of faith I wanted to have. I had a deep desire for humility and to be of service. Being of service came easy for me. It was the humility and meekness I struggled with. Injustice and evil in the world brought out the greatest impatience and intolerance in me. I wanted to be more understanding of people and not interrupt before they could explain themselves fully. And above everything, I desired a pure heart, and I wanted most of all to see my God.

I learned so much from Jesus during this time about what it meant to be one of God's children. Jesus seemed to focus on how we should treat each other. This was something that I had struggled with at different times in my life. Whenever I faced injustice of any kind, I tended to strike out without thinking, especially when it involved children and the elderly of our town. I could often let my anger get the better of me and knew I needed to temper it. I was prone to speak before thinking, and it usually got me in trouble, and sometimes my language did not suit that of the woman of faith I professed to be. I wanted to tame my tongue and worked on it with my biggest praying. I prayed about all this often in my journals. Jesus preached love to his people. God had so much love to share that it only seemed right that we should show as much love as we could to others.

But this didn't mean that life was always easy for Jesus and his disciples. On the contrary, many times they found themselves locked up in jail for one reason or another. Typically, the charges were thin at best, but the dissent against Jesus's teachings was beginning to grow, and it became harder and harder to ignore what was being said.

When Mary and I went to the market, we would often overhear conversations. Many people praised Jesus and wondered who he was that he was so favored by God. But others questioned his authority and the things he was saying. They did not believe him to be the son of God and cried heresy for claiming such. Some even said he was no son of God and instead was the son of evil.

John the Baptist was arrested by King Herod himself for speaking on Jesus's behalf. When we got word that he had been beheaded, I fell to my knees in grief. Such a rough end for such a strong and faithful man. The news nearly broke Mary as she mourned for the pain her cousin Elizabeth must have felt at the sad news. She regretted not being near Elizabeth to ease her suffering. We prayed for Elizabeth that evening.

I asked God why this had to happen to John. Why would his faithful servant meet such an end? I received the same reassurance as I had when Joseph passed away. John was now with God in the kingdom of Heaven. He was safe from harm and sorrow. He had fulfilled his purpose on earth and died glorifying God. There was no greater calling than that.

I felt as though I failed daily in my faith to God. I questioned him constantly and doubted the ways of the world, but God always saw me through. It was a daily struggle for me to be as humble and to set a good example. My truest heart's desire was to be as much like Jesus as I could. I wanted to love like he loved, unconditionally and with no expectations. I looked to Mary often in my daily walk to see how a woman of The Way should act. She never lost faith and never questioned God no matter what happened. She still was a big help in tempering my quick response and anger as well. She had truly become my role model. Mary was a woman of great faith—just what I wanted to be. I could feel God creating in me a new heart—that pure heart I desired.

I questioned her about how she was able to remain faithful in the midst of everything she'd been through, especially now as we heard all the terrible things people were saying about her son. She reminded me of the day she was visited by the angel of God. She said yes to him that day and has continued to say yes to him every day. She told me of a conversation she had with Elizabeth during their visit. She said something to Elizabeth then and had been praying it ever since. I asked her about that prayer.

"It's simple really. 'My soul proclaims the greatness of the Lord, and my spirit rejoices in God my savior. For he has looked upon his handmaid's lowliness, behold, from now on will all ages call me blessed. The Mighty One has done great things for me and holy is his name. His mercy is from age to age to those who fear him. He has shown might with his arm, dispersed the arrogant of mind and heart. He has thrown down the rulers from their thrones but lifted up the lowly. The hungry he has filled with good things; the rich he has sent away empty. He has helped Israel his servant, remembering his mercy, according to his promise to our fathers, Abraham and to his descendants forever."[2] I pray this often, and it gives me courage to stand faithful to God my Father and to Jesus my son. Gee, you should write your own prayer too. Write something to God that says all the things you believe and love about him," Mary replied in her humble yet suggestive way that was always irresistible to me.

"I do write many of my thoughts to God in my journals, Mary. I'll think about your prayer though and see if I can come up with one of my own like that—maybe it will help me to stand faithful like you," I said, already thinking of a start of this prayer. I truly wanted to be a woman of faith and worked hard to overcome my weaknesses. I wanted God to see to the intentions of my heart and not hold me accountable for some of my actions.

---

2   Luke 1:46–55

I was greatly tested when I was trying to sell one of my linens to a merchant. As Jesus's ministry grew, he began to travel farther and farther. Mary and I were finding it harder to keep up with him and would sometimes stay home, so I took up my weaving again. It was a joy to see what my fingers could remember, and I used it to glorify God and his ministry as well. My fingers were often guided by God as I deftly moved the shuttle in and out of the loom, creating beautiful pictures of Jesus as he preached as well as embroidered teachings he had given to me; "Stand Faithful" and "Pray Big" was one of my favorite designs to weave. I used every opportunity I could to share the word, even in my needlework.

Mary had gone to the market with me to meet with a merchant who was interested in buying some linen for his wife as a present. I had met him during one of the gatherings when his wife commented on the fine detail of Mary's and my robes. It was simple, but she still noticed the craftwork that went into making it. Afterward, the man sought me out to see if I would make a similar garment for his wife to which I eagerly agreed. I took an instant liking to both of them and felt proud to share my gifts. The money it would bring would help with food for us and the others who traveled with us.

The man had a business located in the middle of town. When we arrived, he was haggling with another customer over a price, so I waited patiently for him to finish. As we waited, Mary and I began to look through some of the other wares. There was a group of men who were seated next to the stall and arguing loudly. It was impossible to not overhear.

"I don't know who this Jesus thinks he is, but he is no son of God," an old man with white hair said. He was dressed in ornate robes of the brightest purple I had ever seen. The threading was in gold, and I could tell that he was wealthy. His two colleagues were also richly dressed, but it was clear that they deferred to the old man.

"Have you heard him speak?" one of the younger men asked. "His words seem sound. There is authority behind what he preaches."

The old man spat on the ground in disgust. "There are always pretenders."

"What about the miracles they say he has performed? I heard he brought a man back from the dead."

"A trick, I say. He is no more the son of God than I am. And I'm not the only one who feels this way. It's heresy for him to go around claiming these things. I've never seen him cure somebody of as much as a cough. Bring the dead back to life, bah!"

I was beginning to feel anger rise as I overheard all of this and suddenly could not hold my tongue. I went right up to the old man and said, "Excuse me. What do you know

about Jesus? You don't even know him! Let me tell you—"
Before I could continue, I felt Mary's hand pulling me away
from the group of men.

"Gee, no," Mary said. She held my shoulder and tried to
pull me away. "Do not do this here."

I turned to her in astonishment. "Did you hear what
they said?" I asked, willing myself to lower my voice. "I can't
stand by and listen to this."

"I know, but do not speak against them in anger. It will
only fuel their hate. Come back when you can speak from
a place of love."

I heard the truth in her words and bowed my head to the
group of men. "I'm sorry for disturbing you." I went to the
other side of the stall and bit back all of my bad thoughts. I
said a quiet prayer to God to give me strength and humility. I didn't want to spread hate or anger. That wasn't what
Jesus would have wanted. I quickly finished the transaction
with the merchant and headed home. I didn't want to give
myself the chance to hear any other words against Jesus in
my volatile state. I vowed, once again, to stand faithful in
spite of myself.

But that wasn't the last we would hear against Jesus. The
more followers Jesus seemed to gain, the more outcriers
there were. And the threats against Jesus and his disciples
became harsher. The talk was becoming more and more
frightening for me to hear, and I knew how distressing it

was to Mary. We prayed daily, but the fear was growing in our hearts. Neither of us would say it out loud, but we felt as though there were something coming, something we wouldn't be able to stop.

Mary brought her fears to Jesus that evening as we sat for the evening meal. She knew the only person who could assuage them was her beloved son. "Have you heard the rumors?" she asked him. "Have you heard what they say against you? What can we do?"

Jesus was wise beyond his years now, no longer the curious little boy. He was a man with his own mind and his own heart. He knew what needed to be done, and he was willing to shoulder the burden. He smiled at his mother and took her hands in his. "Everything is going according to God's plan," he reassured her. "Mother, trust in him who sent me."

"I shall do as you ask, son," Mary whispered.

Then Jesus turned those eyes on me. Those eyes were deeper than the ocean. "Gee, you will need to stand faithful as well. Will you be a rock for my mother to lean on? And another thing, don't stop praying big like you do. Pray big for me, Gee."

"I too will do as you ask, I promise, son," I repeated Mary's words. There were tears in my eyes as I said the word I had always associated with him. I felt as though he could have been of my own flesh as well. I loved him like a son, but I also knew he was much more than that to me. He was my Messiah. He smiled at me in a way that I knew things would be okay, somehow.

But that fear was still there.

13

Then he took the bread, said the blessing,
broke it, and gave it to them saying,
"This is my body, which will be given for you;
do this in memory of me.
And likewise the cup after they had eaten, saying,
"This cup is the new covenant in my blood,
which will be shed for you.

—Luke 22:19–20

JESUS CONTINUED PREACHING, but the atmosphere in some towns and talk among the church elders had definitely changed. There was something sinister in the air as he gained followers. I feared for him and the other disciples. I renewed my own vow to follow his words and stand faithful. I only wished that I could make his enemies see the errors of their ways, and hear the truth Jesus was presenting to them.

His followers were totally devoted to him. Though each of his disciples withstood frequent persecution, it was becoming harder for the world to deny the truth Jesus was preaching. Passover was approaching. Mary and I did not make our usual preparations to celebrate the festivities. Mary said to me, "I feel as though I need to stay close to Jesus. There is so much for him to do."

I agreed. It wouldn't be much of a feast without him there. But then I heard word from some of our friends that they were going to prepare the Passover feast for Jesus and his twelve disciples. We had never done anything like this before, and I eagerly told Mary about it.

"The ladies are going to make bread and prepare the meal. Peter and John found a house with a large upper room. Peter said that Jesus instructed them to have the feast. He has never asked for anything like this before."

"Do not worry," Mary said. "Whatever it is, Jesus will tell us in due time."

"Are you going to come help?"

Mary closed her eyes and thought about it for a minute. "No, I think I will spend the night in prayer. You are welcome to join me."

I knew I should. She was my dearest friend who had never steered me wrong before, but I felt so anxious and curious. I knew that I would not be able to sit still in prayer for very long. My curiosity would surely get the better of me. I told Mary that I would go to the house and see if I could help with preparations for Jesus's supper.

When I arrived, the kitchen was already bustling with women as they prepared the feast. I immediately rolled up my sleeves and began to chop up carrots and onions.

"I brought a tablecloth, one of my finest," I said to no one in particular. There was very little talk in the kitchen, and I had to fill the void. "I didn't know if there was already one here." I pointed to the basket I had brought with me, and a woman walked over to examine it closer.

"There is one upstairs already, but it is quite plain. I'm sure no one would mind if we replaced it. Yours is quite beautiful," a woman said. "I'm Sarah. When you finish up, we can go upstairs and begin setting the table before Jesus and his disciples arrive."

I introduced myself to Sarah and quickly finished my task and picked up my basket to carry upstairs. In it, I had neatly folded my finest linen. I had been working on this piece of cloth for some time without knowing for what purpose it would be used. It had an intricate scroll design along the border in the softest silk thread I owned. I had only finished it the week before and tucked it away while I thought about what to use it for. When I heard about the supper, I knew that this was the reason I had made it.

The upstairs room was spacious with a long wooden table up in the center. A stack of dishes was on a sideboard. I looked at the old tablecloth and pinched the fabric between my fingers. It was rough and woolen with numerous stains. "This won't do at all," I said as I began to fold the old one to put away. "The son of God deserves so much more. Not that my handiwork is much to brag about, but at the very least, he deserves clean linen. Jesus deserves the best we can offer, and that is what I want for him. I guess I'm still greedy for him."

Sarah looked at me puzzled. "What do you man you are greedy for him?"

"If God has a blessing for Jesus, I pray that God will give him two blessings. I want all good things for him, a lot of good things. I want him to have everything that God has planned for him and not miss out on any good thing. I used to feel the same way about my husband, Eli. God rest his soul. He died many years ago. I was greedy for him too. I wanted him to be blessed by God over and over. Do you see what I mean?"

Sarah looked at me and nodded. "Yes, Gertrude, I think I do. I'm greedy for those I love too. I want them to have all of God's blessings too. This kind of greed is good, not the kind of greed we see on the streets among the merchants," she replied with a smile.

"Yes, it sure is. Maybe greedy isn't the right word to use, but it's my little way of saying how I feel about those whom I love," I replied.

I hadn't realized I was just rambling away. I was still feeling anxious as I spread that beautiful linen across the large table. It fit perfectly, and I was amazed.

"Do you know him well? Jesus I mean," Sarah asked.

"Oh, I do. I've known him since his birth."

"Have you always known about him?"

"In some ways. He's always been such a bright and special boy. He was quiet and kept to himself mostly, but he was always there to help when I needed it. But he quickly showed us how smart and faithful he was. I didn't always understand that he was the son of God or what exactly that meant, but I knew he was destined for greatness."

Sarah grew quiet as we began to lay out the place settings. Thirteen plates were arranged with thirteen of the best cups we could gather. We laid out utensils and then brought up the jugs of wine while the rest of the meal was being prepared.

"I feel as though this supper is important somehow," Sarah said when we finished and stood back to admire our work. "I can't quite explain the feeling deep in my heart, but I know I will never forget this night. I've listened to his teachings and feel my heart stir whenever he speaks. I'm a believer, Gertrude, and I want to follow what he teaches."

"I feel the same way. Tonight does seem different somehow. I'm so happy that you heard Jesus talk and believe. God will honor your intentions, Sarah. Sometimes we want to do the right thing and fail. I think God knows our true intentions and honors them as long as we are following him," I said and grabbed her hand to squeeze. "His mother, Mary, decided to stay home and pray. Maybe I should have listened to her and done the same, but I wanted to help with the meal, and I feel the need to see Jesus tonight. I want to see for myself that he is okay."

"Why don't we pray for a minute while the other women finish up downstairs and before the men arrive?"

"Thank you," I said. We fell to our knees in that finely decorated room and prayed to God. Neither of us really knew what to pray for because we couldn't quite identify the strange feelings we were both having. We ended up praying for peace and guidance to do what was right and to stand faithful to God's decisions.

When we stood up, I felt how much I had aged over the years. My knees throbbed from the hard flooring, and my back hurt a great deal from bending forward in prayer. It seemed like only yesterday I was a young wife with the whole world in front of me. Now I was an old lady, passing into my later years of life. My hair was graying at the temples, and the skin was loose on the backs of my hands. I still felt young in my spirit though. I could still engage with others about God and the teachings of Jesus as if I were only twenty, but at the end of the day, I eased into bed with care and had to acknowledge the aches and pains of an aging woman. I woke each morning thankful that God had given me another day.

I was startled from my reminiscing by a call up the stairs: "They're arriving!"

Sarah and I both checked over the room once more and then went downstairs to begin bringing up the food. I grabbed a bowl of fresh fruit to carry up. On my way back down, I nearly ran over one of the disciples coming upstairs. "Judas! My goodness, I am so sorry for running into you like that."

"Not to worry. I'm okay," he answered, but he didn't look me in the eye. Judas often had a smile for me but not this night.

"Is everything all right?"

His eyes shifted to my face but quickly looked away again. I couldn't quite read the different emotions that were playing across his face. "Yes, everything is fine. I'm just looking forward to the meal, that's all."

He moved past me and nervously continued up the stairs. I let his odd behavior go. This was an unusual night, and everyone seemed to sense it. An atmosphere of antic-ipation filled the air. I came downstairs and found Jesus standing before. He looked more beautiful than ever. He was smiling to the other women and thanking them for their work. Then his eyes found me.

"Gee, thank you for your work," he said to me and kissed me on the forehead. He stood much taller than I now.

"I just wanted to see your face, beloved," I replied. I kissed his hands and had one last look as he led the rest of his followers upstairs.

The other women set about to cleaning and gossiping after the last disciples disappeared up the staircase. I was too curious. I grabbed an extra wine jug and followed quietly up the stairs. I knew I shouldn't eavesdrop on their dinner, but I was too curious. I wanted to know more about Jesus and the significance of this night, so I climbed the stairs quietly and stood in the doorway where I peeked through a crack into the room.

Jesus wasn't seated at the head of the table as I had expected but rather in the middle. That was typical of him, quick to fit in rather than stand out. Though, honestly, he always stood out for one reason or another. The men quieted down, and all looked to Jesus before they reached for any bowls. He said to them, "I have eagerly desired to eat this Passover with you before I suffer, for, I tell you, I shall not eat it again until there is fulfillment in the kingdom of God."

What does this mean? I wondered. Surely, he can't fast for that long. He had fasted forty days in the desert, but this could be years. I also didn't know what he meant by "fulfillment."

Jesus picked up a cup, gave thanks, and said, "Take this and share it among yourselves; for I tell you that from this time on, I shall not drink of the fruit of the vine until the kingdom of God comes." Then he took the bread, said the blessing, broke it, and gave it to them, saying, "This is my body, which will be given for you; do this in memory of me." And likewise, he took the cup after they had eaten, saying, "This cup is the new covenant in my blood, which will be shed for you."

The cup and the bread passed around the table. Each man took a sip of the wine and tore off a piece of the bread. They did this somberly though I caught a few glances that were shared among them. Clearly, I wasn't the only one who was confused by these actions. After they partook in the covenant, they began to feast.

I hadn't seen Jesus take a single bite, and after a long while, he spoke again. "And yet behold, the hand of the one who is to betray me is with me on the table; for the Son of Man indeed goes as it has been determined; but woe to that man by whom he is betrayed." And they began to debate among themselves who among them would do such a deed.[1]

---

[1] Luke 22:14–23

Their voices reached such a pitch that I was in shock. I had never seen these men act in such a way. It was hard for me to believe that one of them could betray their beloved Jesus either. I felt the tears come to my eyes, and I knew I should leave. I should not have come at all. I ran down the stairs and left the jug in the kitchen. I didn't even bother to say good-bye to the women. I ran all the way home despite my age. I went inside and barred the door behind me.

I moved quietly through the house, afraid to wake Mary, but she was still awake by the fire, praying. I fell in beside her and let the sobs take over. She leaned into me and wrapped me in a comforting hug as she prayed over me. Each time I tried to start an apology, to tell her how wrong I was to go that night, that I should've stayed faithful with her, she shushed me.

I didn't know when it happened, but eventually, I fell asleep right there on the floor with my head in her lap.

14

Then he opened their minds to
understand the scriptures."
And he said to them, "Thus it is written
that the Messiah would suffer
and rise from the dead on the third day
and that repentance for the forgiveness of sins
would be preached in his name
to all the nations, beginning from Jerusalem.
You are witnesses to these things.

—Luke 24:45–48 (NAB)

IN THE MORNING, we were disturbed by a loud knock at the door. It was John, panting and out of breath. "Come in, come in," I ushered him and he collapsed in a chair. "What has happened?"

Mary came bustling into the kitchen to see what all the noise was about.

"He's been arrested," John finally gasped.

"Who? Who's been arrested?" Mary asked, her hand to her heart.

"Jesus" was all he said.

Mary sat down heavily in a chair.

"Are you sure?" I asked. "Are you sure it is Jesus who has been arrested? What are the charges?"

"They claim he is inciting the people to revolt," John replied.

"That's ridiculous!" I said. "No one could believe that our gentle Jesus would do such a thing. He only wants to bring believers into the kingdom of his father. He preaches love and respect, not violence and anarchy. Surely, the charges won't stick." My temper was already starting to flare, but one look from John, and I could see the truth in his news. I didn't want to believe it. But then I realized that what I had heard last night about him being betrayed must have really happened. What could that mean for Jesus's life?

"Thank you, John," Mary said. She stood up and hugged him before he left. After the door closed, Mary turned to me and said, "God's word must be fulfilled."

"What does that mean?" I asked, incredulous as her calmness.

"It means we should pray."

"Whom or what should we pray for? Mary, I'll go to the officials. Maybe I can convince them that Jesus is innocent.

I will make them understand they have the wrong man!"
I cried.

"Oh, Gee, I know you would go, but you must remain
here. There will be many distraught souls in the days to come.
Many will need forgiveness, so we should pray for them."

She was speaking so cryptically. Again, I marveled at
her faith—to pray at a time like this? All I wanted to do
was go to the officials and fight for Jesus's release. Instead, I
chose to overcome my natural tendency and follow Mary's
example. Now, I would stand faithful. We prayed all the rest
of the day and into the night. We did not rest but to share
a meager midday meal, and we went to bed late into the
night only to wake early and begin our prayers anew. We
waited to hear news, any news, about what was happening
with Jesus. One of the disciples would stop in periodically
to give us any updates. First, we were told that Jesus was
before the Sanhedrin for trial, but then he was sent on to
Pontius Pilate.

I felt a renewed sense of hope at this. Surely Pilate would
see how outrageous these charges were, but the people were
crying for death. He was such an even-tempered man with
a heart for justice. After Pilate, Jesus was sent before King
Herod, and I was worried. He was a descendant of the
man who sought to kill Jesus in infancy, but again, Jesus
was sent back to Pilate's court. I wondered if this were all

just some cruel farce, meant to send fear into the hearts of Jesus's followers.

Finally, in the early evening, John returned more distraught than ever.

"Please, just tell us," I begged.

"Death."

I burst into tears, but Mary managed to maintain her composure. "What happened?" she asked.

"Pilate found no charges against him and wanted only to flog him and release him. But the people were in a frenzy. They wanted more. Pilate gave them the option of freeing a man who was actually convicted of murder or freeing Jesus." John dropped his head into his hands. "They chose the murderer, Barabbas. Jesus will be crucified on the morrow."

"We must pray," was all Mary said.

I could barely speak as the sobs racked my body. I didn't even notice when John left the house. Mary and I enveloped each other into a hug as I felt the tears streaming down her cheeks. Only God would give us the strength to make it through tomorrow. I had to keep reminding myself that this must be all part of God's plan for our redemption like Jesus had told me. This was the fulfillment of the prophecies. Jesus was going to his death to save people like me from eternal damnation. But he was like a lamb to the slaughter, and I couldn't help but to picture that tiny baby who opened my heart to true understanding.

In the morning, we put on our heavy veils and made our way into the city. It wasn't hard to know where to go. People had come in droves to witness the spectacle. The path Jesus would take was already blocked off. I wanted to turn away when I first caught sight of Jesus coming down the road. He was carrying his heavy wooden cross over his back, and the weight of it made him hunch forward.

"We must be witnesses, Gertrude," Mary said to me when I started to turn my head to the side. "Now is the time to truly stand faithful."

I looked back, and Jesus had drawn closer. I could see the full extent of his suffering, blood streaming down his face from where soldiers had put a crown of thorns on his head in mockery. There were whiplashes all across his back that also wept blood, but somehow, Jesus found the strength to move on. It was a long way to go to the top of the hill, Golgotha. I didn't know how he would make it. Jesus stumbled in front of us but managed to get up in spite of the crack of a whip for the third time. But when he stumbled again, he wasn't able to lift the cross again. The guards pulled a man from the crowd and bade him to pick up the cross for Jesus. After that, the progress continued.

It was hard to watch, but Mary and I followed him the rest of the way. The crowd seemed to always make room for us to get by and keep pace with our beloved. Finally, the hill loomed in the distance, and we all seemed to breathe a sigh of relief that the end of suffering was near. I would not turn away no matter how much my heart rent in two. I vowed to myself and to my beloved Jesus that I would watch and I would witness. I would not look away from his Passion suffered for me.

When we reached the place called the Skull, they crucified him and two criminals there, one on his right, the other on his left. Then Jesus said, "Father, forgive them. They know not what they do."

They divided his garments by casting lots. The people stood by and watched; the rulers, meanwhile, sneered at him and said, "He saved others. Let him save himself if he is the chosen one, the Messiah of God."

Even the soldiers jeered at him. As they approached to offer him wine, they called out, "If you are King of the Jews, save yourself." Above him there was an inscription that read, "This is the King of the Jews."

Now one of the criminals hanging there reviled Jesus, saying, "Are you not the Messiah? Save yourself and us."

The other, however, rebuking him, said in reply, "Have you no fear of God, for you are subject to the same condemnation? And indeed, we have been condemned justly, for the sentence we received corresponds to our crimes, but this man has done nothing criminal." Then he said, "Jesus, remember me when you come into your kingdom."

Jesus replied to him, "Amen, I say to you, today you will be with me in Paradise."

It was now about noon, and darkness came over the whole land until three in the afternoon because of an eclipse of the sun. Then the veil of the temple was torn down the middle. Jesus cried out in a loud voice, "Father, into your hands I commend my spirit." And when he had said this, he breathed his last.

I overheard the centurion, who witnessed what had happened, glorify God by saying, "This man was innocent beyond doubt."

After a long while, the people who had gathered for this spectacle returned home. Mary and I and the rest of his followers present stood at a distance.[1] I couldn't believe my eyes. This bright, beautiful boy was now bloody and dead. He was counted among criminals and had met the cruelest fate possible. I was so stunned that the tears would no longer come. There were no words to express my sorrow.

Mary and I stayed there until Jesus's body was taken down. A man, Joseph of Arimathea, assured us that he had a tomb prepared to lay Jesus in. He would not allow Jesus

---

1   Luke 23:33–49

become a feast for carrion birds. Joseph was a secret follower of the Way of Jesus and had procured permission to bury Jesus in a tomb he already had.

As Jesus's body lay in Mary's arms, she wept over him. I will never forget the look on her face. I realized at that moment that she had suffered along with him—for all of us who would belong to him. She stayed there for a long moment, joining her suffering with his. My heart ached for yet another mother, my friend, Mary, holding her dead son.

"Oh, Gee, they have killed my son." Mary cried, rocking back and forth holding her son.

We went home after the body had been wrapped in linen, placed in the tomb, and the stone rolled in place closing it. We walked home, hand in hand.

"Gee, I remember what Simeon said to me when we presented Jesus in the temple. He said a sword would pierce my heart. I know what he meant. I feel that sword piercing my heart just when the soldier pierced Jesus's side. I felt his pain. You know, when I said yes to the angel, I surely never thought it would end this way," Mary said somberly.

I wondered how I could possibly comfort my friend at a time like this. I remembered my own grief at losing both of my children. A mother should never have to bury her children, and certainly not like this. When we arrived at home, I helped her get ready for bed and held her until she fell asleep. Mary had become the friend I'd prayed for and had become my family. I knew we were meant to find each other for just a moment as this. I was grateful to God for sending me to this woman and her family. I would stand faithful to her now in her time of need. We were both widows, and now we were both childless mothers. Our bond was deep and true.

Just as the sun was coming out on Sunday morning, some of the women came to our door with some incredible news. They had gone to anoint Jesus's body, but something miraculous had happened. "He's gone," they said.

"Gone? What do you mean? How can he be gone?" I asked, thinking they were made with grief.

"We went to the tomb, and the stone was moved. There was no way a single man could have moved that stone. The burial shroud was still in the cave, but Jesus's body was gone."

I looked to Mary and saw her smiling. I didn't understand. "Let us go and find the disciples," Mary said. I was in shock, but I listened. We formed up in a line and followed Mary from the house. It wasn't hard to find the men gathered together, and the women shared their tale with them as well. They didn't understand what was going on either.

Then suddenly, Jesus appeared to our group. He said, "Peace be with you."

I nearly jumped out of my skin I was so terrified. I couldn't believe my eyes. Standing before me was the perfect body of Jesus. I thought I was seeing a ghost, but he looked so real. Surely this wasn't a trick of my imagination. As I looked around the group, I knew I wasn't the only one seeing this apparition. The only person who was not surprised by his appearance was Mary. She had tears in her eyes as she gazed at her holy son. The disciples were backing away.

Then he said to them, "Why are you troubled? And why do questions arise in your hearts? Look at my hands and my feet, that it is I myself. Touch me and see, because a ghost does not have flesh and bones as you can see I have." And as he said this, he showed them his hands and his feet. While they stood in astonishment, he asked them, "Have you anything here to eat?" They gave him a piece of baked fish; he took it and ate it in front of them.

He said to them, "These are my words that I spoke to you while I was still with you, that everything written about me in the Law of Moses and in the prophets and psalms must be fulfilled." Then he opened their minds to understand the scriptures. And he said to them, "Thus it is written that the Messiah would suffer and rise from the dead on the third day and that repentance, for the forgiveness of sins, would be preached in his name to all the nations, beginning from Jerusalem. You are witnesses of these things. And, behold, I am sending the promise of my Father upon you; but stay in the city until you are clothed with power from on high."

He appeared several more times in the next days. Two men traveling to Emmaus told of sharing a meal with a man as they recognized him to be Jesus.

Jesus appeared one late afternoon as I was sitting in my garden writing my prayers. I was immediately humbled that he would reveal himself to me.

"Gee, I see you are still praying big, just as I've asked. I love you, daughter. You still have much to do for my Father's kingdom. Stand faithful and be willing always to work hard for he who sent me. You will receive my Holy Spirit along with the others. He is the one who will help you to overcome your flesh and live in harmony with the will of the Father. Ask me for what you need, my dear sweet Gee. I cannot resist your clean, pure heart. You bring me great joy. Your joy will be boundless in the life I promise you. Well done, my good and faithful daughter."

"Jesus, I still have questions. Won't you stay for a little while?" I pleaded

"What would you have me tell you, my daughter?" He answered.

"Jesus, my Lord. You have always been able to look me in the eye, even when I was not looking directly at you, and you help me to be honest about things. That's why I love you so much. It's that no-kidding-around thing about you, and it's all in your eyes. I knew your eyes were special the moment I first saw them after you were born. Lord, tell me about my Father in heaven."

"Oh, Gee, you want to know about the Father, your Father? Oh, my daughter, he has been waiting a long time for you to want to be with him. I've told him, "She will come, she's stubborn, just like we made her. It might take a while, she's been hurt, and her pain runs deep. But she will come.'"

Jesus continued, "I can tell you, it pained him to see your broken heart. We know how hard Satan tried to convince you to stay in your pain. Many prayed for you to be remain strong and faithful. Like my mother, your earthly mother prayed for your safety. Their intercession was mighty, and he heard them and delivered you. "

I am overwhelmed at what I am hearing Jesus say to my heart. Our conversation was so intimate. "I have prayed to the Father for many years. Sometimes he answers, and sometimes it seems he is silent. Does he really hear me when I call to him?"

"Oh yes, Gee, he hears. He hears all who call upon him. He answers all prayers. It may not always seem to be what you desire, but trust him for what is best for your soul always. His love for you, our love for you, knows no bounds and will never leave you. Trust us and fear nothing, my beloved." Jesus answers softly.

"There is one more thing, my Jesus. The supper, the last supper you shared with your disciples before they took you.

I don't understand it. What does it all mean?" I asked, my curiosity winning out again.

"In human terms, it may be bread and wine, but on divine terms, my terms, it becomes my sacrifice again—just for you. It becomes that which brings you salvation, hope, and the ability to love. I have given this supper to renew and refresh believers. When you feel my voice has lost its clarity, become faint or feel distant, this meal I have given will make all things clear again. This is how you will keep our relationship strong and sustained. Partake of it often in remembrance of me and my sacrifice offered for you. Thank you for asking about this." He answered as he slowly stepped away from me.

Before I could speak another word, he simply vanished before my eyes. I stayed there on my bench and wrote all he had said. Joy expanded my heart as tears streamed down my face. I wondered what it was I still had to do for the Father's kingdom. Whatever it was, I told him my response would be yes, even before he revealed it to me.

A few days later, he appeared again and led all of us out as far as Bethany, raised his hands, and blessed us. As he blessed us, he parted from us and was taken up to heaven. We did him homage and then returned to Jerusalem with great joy.[2] I wanted to shout from the rooftops that the

---

2   Luke 24:36–53

Messiah had returned to us and fulfilled the prophecy. I wanted to tell all of the nonbelievers that the only way to God was through Christ our savior.

"We will tell them," Mary said to me when I explained how much my heart wanted to jump out of my chest for joy. "We stood witness to this miracle and the fulfillment of the prophecy. Now we will praise his name until our dying breaths so that the world will know he is—King in Heaven."

My heart was heavy with grief over the death of this man whom I had loved from the day of his birth. It was also light with the joy of knowing he was truly the Messiah. He was my Messiah, my Lord, and my Savior, and I would stand faithful to him for the rest of my life.

15

When Jesus saw his mother
and the disciple there whom he loved,
he said to his mother, "Woman, behold, your son."
Then he said to the disciple,
"Behold, your mother."
And from that hour
the disciple took her into his home.

—John: 26–27 (NAB)

FROM THE CROSS, Jesus had told John to behold his mother. John took those words to his heart. Mary and I went with John to his home and lived there. We filled our days with prayer, weaving and remembering our times with Jesus. Everyone was eager to hear Mary talk about her son. The disciples each went on their journeys spreading the good news of Jesus and teaching his way. Many people came to believe because of their preaching.

Many months had gone by when I began noticing Mary's appetite diminishing. She no longer had the energy to weave for very long and tired very easily. Mary was growing weaker, and I could see her health failing. I was with her as she lay in bed one morning, too weak to rise.

"Stay in bed today, Mary, I will bring you some tea. The rest will do you good," I urged.

"Yes, Gee. Tea would be good," she replied, without protest.

I prepared the tea and a small meal for her. I thought she was asleep with I returned, but she opened her eyes as I entered the room.

"Gertrude, you have been such a dear friend to me all these years. I wonder if you realize how much you mean to me. Do you remember when we met? I was so afraid that night when Joseph brought us to the inn. You made me feel safe. You knew just what to do."

"Oh, Mary, don't talk, you will wear yourself out. Rest." I could barely talk through my tears. How well did I remember that night? It changed the course of my life.

"Gee, I must tell you before it's too late. You and I have been blessed to have found each other. I am so sorry that you lost your precious Eli. I know how much you loved him. I hope that your pain was lessened by living with us. We loved you so much. I love you so much. I spoke to Jesus often about you. I knew your struggles with your temper, your way of telling people the first thing that comes to your mind. And, Gee, that tongue of yours. I told Jesus not to hold any of it against you. You are so full of life. You always have been. You have a zest for living that Jesus and I always loved. You lived big, you loved big, and I know that you pray big. I think that is what made your prayers so irresistible to God and to our Jesus."

"Mary, you make too much of me. I'm such a sinner. I try to do the right thing, but it seems it doesn't always work out that way. I want you to know, my dear friend, that I have loved you since that night in the stable. Helping you to birth Jesus is the most beautiful and worthwhile thing I have ever done. I must confess to you though that I was green with envy when you first arrived. I had lost my babies, and there you were having one that lived and was so beautiful. You helped me to overcome that sin, and for that I am forever grateful. I am so happy you let me help you that night. And truth be known, I was scared too. I thank you, Mary, for overlooking my faults and accepting me into your family." I was feeling so much love; I thought my heart would burst.

"My sweet friend, you were meant to be with us. It was God's plan that you become one of Jesus's followers. All I was supposed to do was help to make him known to you. When I offered him to you as a baby, I remember that you hesitated, but only for a quick moment. You accepted my son so eagerly and have been accepting him every day since that night. This was my purpose—to help you to meet him and come to know and love him. His purpose has been fulfilled—to make way that we can all be together again in our Father's kingdom. And now, Gertrude, my dear, it's time for you to fulfill your purpose," she said as her breath grew weaker.

"Wait, Mary, wait! My purpose, what is my purpose? Tell me," I said, anxious for her to say more. But she had fallen asleep. It would have to wait. I went quickly to retrieve my journal scroll and began to pray. *O Lord, please let me have her for a while longer. You have blessed me so much with her friendship. I am so grateful for all you have done for me. It is all much more than I deserve, and yet you love me anyway. Help me to discern clearly what my purpose is. What is it you would have me do?*

As I sipped tea and finished my meal, I heard Mary stirring and went to her. She was very weak, and I sensed the end was near.

"Gee, did I tell you? Did I speak of God's purpose for you?" she whispered softly.

"No, Mary, you didn't. You fell asleep. But not to worry. I've asked God to reveal it to me, and I'm certain he will in time. You rest now."

"But I must tell you. In my dreams, he revealed it to me. You must continue to pray big as you always have. And, Gee, please keep writing. Your journals will one day be a witness for others who come behind you. There will be those who will never have the chance to know you or the life you lived with Eli and with me, Joseph, and Jesus. They will never know of the things you've learned about how to love the way he taught. You can tell them by the way your heart loves to pray—in your journals," she said growing weaker.

"I will, Mary, I promise I will keep writing my prayers. I will write all about us and our life together. I will write about how we met and came to be a family. Have I thanked you enough for accepting me when I followed you out of Bethlehem? I am so grateful. I was lost after Eli's death at the hand of Herod's soldiers. You gave me a reason to keep living. Mary, thank you for loving me. Thank you for giving your son to me. I am so glad I accepted him that night in the stable. You made it so easy to grow in my faith. You have always been a great example for me to follow." The tears were streaming down my face, but I realized they were not tears of sorrow but those of joy. Each drop was bursting with love and happiness over the life I have had.

"I hope my example will lead you to my son, Jesus. That has been my purpose always. I will ask him to watch over you when I join him in our Father's kingdom."

"Mary, no, not yet," I cried.

"Gee, do you remember the prayer I told you about that I wrote when I visited my cousin Elizabeth? Read it often, pray it, and then write your own prayer—one that shows all you believe. I will pray for you, my friend. I love you, Gee," she said as she breathed her last.

"Oh, Mary." I held her in my arms and cried for yet another loss. I knew in my heart that she was with her husband, Joseph, and with her son, Jesus. The peace of this knowledge strengthened me in a profound way. I stood and called out to John. As he walked into the room, we both noticed something strange happening. Was her body beginning to rise?

16

My Little Magnificat

My soul dances with joy at the sound
of the Father calling my name.
I go to Him, unafraid and trusting, and rest myself.
I am home at last.
Thank you my Jesus, my Christ,
for making the way that I might
delight in my Father's company.
You, O Lord, are my salvation,
my refuge, my sanctuary.
No enemy can reach me as long as I remain with you.
It is in you alone, my Heavenly Father,
that I place my trust and my hope.
It is you I love.
You satisfy every desire of my heart.
I want to worship you all the days of my life.

Let me never be put to shame because
my sin has come between us.
Show me your ways Father.
Show me your heart.
Let all that I am love you more each day.
I desire your will for me Father, Your will.
All this I pray through your Son, Jesus Christ,
my Lord and my Savior.
Amen.

— Joan T Broussard

I LIVED THE rest of my life knowing that at its end, I would be welcomed into the arms of the Father and would once again see the bright, shining face of my beloved Jesus, my friend Mary, and her husband, Joseph. I also have the assurance that I would join Eli and once again hold my babies. This knowledge is a great comfort to me. I did what Mary asked of me and have been writing the story of my life with this holy family. I also wrote my own prayer just like Mary did. I decided to call it "My Little Magnificat" to the Lord.

Mary was the friend and confidant I had prayed for. Joseph was also my friend and brother. Jesus was like a son to me. I helped to bring him into the world by being midwife to his mother. I experienced his healing touch on my body as well as in my spirit. I witnessed his love and his compassion toward those who would kill him. He taught me how to be a woman of faith who could look in the mirror and accept the failings and acknowledge the strengths of the woman who looked back at me. He has given me the courage to ask him to show me the woman he sees when he looks at me. I have the spiritual bravery to see myself as I truly am: a redeemed sinner, a beloved daughter, a woman who stands faithful and prays big.

Jesus is my Christ, my savior, and my intimate Lord now and forever.

PONDER— JOURNAL YOUR RESPONSES

Group Discussion

1. When was the first time you had an experience of God?
2. What was your image of God as a child?
3. What is your image of God now?
4. When you pray, do you pray to God the Father, God the Son, or God the Holy Spirit? Why?
5. How does Jesus communicate to you?
6. List three things God keeps telling you. Is he whispering or shouting?
7. Complete the following phrases:

   Lord, I know that I am a work in progress…
   Sometimes, I pretend to…
   Sometimes, I wear a mask of…

I need to be honest about....
I need to change...

8. What way does your heart love to pray?
9. Journal your prayer to Jesus today—in your own words.
10. Ask Jesus to show you the person he sees when he looks at you.
11. What obstacles keep you from receiving the love of Jesus?
12. How can you overcome those obstacles?
13. List ten things you are grateful for today.
14. Write your *Magnificat*.
15. What is your heart's deepest longing?

APPENDIX

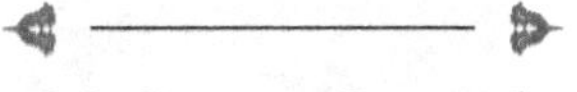

My Retreat Journal

I HAVE ALWAYS believed that our prayers are personal but not private. They should be shared in order to encourage and inspire others to overcome their hesitation and open their hearts to God and his love. It is in this spirit that I offer, for your reflection, the journal I wrote as I experienced the character of Gertrude and her interactions with Mary, Joseph, Jesus and ultimately with the Father. This was the journal of my eight-day silent retreat at the Spirituality Center of Loyola in Azpeitia, Spain, the birthplace of St. Ignatius of Loyola. The retreat center is located next to the Basilica of Ignatius of Loyola which is built over the original home of Ignatius.

One more thing to remember about journaling – sentence structure doesn't matter – content does - the journal presented here is as I wrote it with minimal editing.

The journal entries made in the voice of the Innkeeper's wife, Mary, Jesus and the Father are indicated by their name. The other entries in italics are my prayers in my own voice. It was during the writing of this book that I discovered the name of the innkeeper's wife and her husband.

Spiritual Center of Loyola, Azpeitia, Spain

Thursday, March 27, 2008

We arrive in Madrid, Spain, get our bags and are on our way to Azpeitia. The countryside is beautiful, a lot of hills. Multi-story buildings and apartments look very old. Duh - they are.

Lord, let's talk about grace for this retreat. I pray for the grace to know you even better; grace to pray deeper and feel your presence in my soul. Show me what direction you want to lead me in.

<u>10:00 pm, Retreat Center, Room 223</u>
All settled in. Twin bed is comfortable and warm. Tried to call home, but I don't know how to get an outside line – operator can't speak English. I'll try again tomorrow.

The retreat house is so beautiful. There is a Jesuit house next door – all built around the home of St. Ignatius. I am so anxious to see more the grounds.

Father Mark said mass tonight. Great guy – holy priest. His homily was about a man who was blind. The man went for a walk near his home and got lost. He decided to go stand in the middle of the road and wait for someone to stop, find him and offer assistance. Father Mark suggested we put ourselves in a place where Jesus can find us.....in preparation for the retreat. And this I do.

Lord, I want to find you – and I even more want you to find me. Where in this place of St. Ignatius will we meet?

Friday, March 28, 2008
We leave the retreat center for a walk about the grounds. I feel empty. Not a bad empty but a good empty – very calm, peaceful. I suddenly have an image of Jesus as a boy! I tell him,

Come on Jesus, let's play together. Tell me your secrets and I'll tell you mine.

I can't think of another grace to ask for today except – to know him deeper and feel his love physically, spiritually and emotionally – in a way that will last and not fade when I get home.

<u>11:30 pm</u>
Awesome tour of the home of St. Ignatius. This is the first time I have ever been this close to a Saint – really – it feels very humbling – that I could be walking in the place where a saint lived. Wow!

Saturday, March 29, 2008
We drove to San Sebastian today. Walked on the beach, had lunch and drank a beer at a neat restaurant, Playa de Concha.

I am feeling a lot like the character, Much Afraid, in the book, "Hinds Feel on High Places". I feel as though I don't belong here – I'm not smart like the others on retreat – I don't have a college degree – I don't have a strong spirituality like everyone else. I know it's the devil saying, "Who do you think you are – being here with these priests and nuns. Go back where you belong stupid."

Lord, help me to heal my insecurity, my invisibility.

Daddy never made me feel very special to him. I was just another mouth to feed —one of them lost in the crowd of kids. I'm not sure that he ever really looked at me – ever really knew me. I felt his indifference – whether this is accurate or not – these are my feelings.

My image of God is similar – there are so many others for him to attend to – so many others more worthy of his ear – worthy of his attention. I'm not a bad person – just one lost in the sea of faces.

Journal sketch, Sea of faces

Lord, could you please make something to happen to me that will kindle a passion in my soul that will not fade with the passing of time. Or at least show me how to re-kindle my passion. I am in the middle of the road – come find me please – even in the middle of the sea of faces calling on you.

Sunday, March 30, 2008

This morning we are driving to the shrine of Our Lady of Arantzazu. It is so high up in the mountains. Ignatius made his first all-night vigil here in this same church – in front of this same statue. He asked or her help to keep his love and passion for God and to remain celibate.

The story of our Lady of Arantzazu dates back to 1468, approximately 30 years before Ignatius' birth. A shepherd heard a bell, thought it was a cow bell and went to investigate the sound. He found this little statue in a hawthorn bush with a bell on it, ringing. The statue has been dated to 200 years earlier.

It is said that Our Lady chose to come to these Basque people from this town of Arantzazu in the province of Gipuskoa. They loved her and built the first church in her honor. In 1918, Our Lady of Arantzazu was named the first patron of the Basque people in this area.

The Dominicans and the Franciscans were both located at

the church and cared for the grounds. The pope had to settle their dispute over who was in charge. He assigned care of the church to the Franciscans who still live there and care for the church and grounds.

Statue of Our Lady of Arantzazu

While sitting in church, my thoughts go to Our Lady of Arantzazu.

Mother, where do I fit in the kingdom of your son? What is my purpose? What is my job? How can I feel his gaze upon me? How can I keep my faith fire burning? Can you see me? Your statue is so small, yet you are mighty in the eyes of our Lord. You are truly favored by God. You chose these Basque people to come and visit. Would you please choose me too!!

Teach me how to be in love with God. Teach me how to look in my own mirror and see my sin. I want to see the truth about myself, the ugly, the good, the bad, the neglectful, the forgetful and the proud. Come my little Lady of Arantzazu – come into my heart and stir things up. Let's make a new Joan. I give you permission to go everywhere in my soul and prepare it to be a place worthy of your son, Jesus.

Afternoon

Back at the retreat center – we are beginning our silent retreat today. My director will be Sister Lucy Silvio. At our first spiritual direction session, she asked me to journal about the things I am grateful for, the blessings of the past year and to reflect on Psalm 34: 1-11.

I started my assignment what would become my favorite chapel, Oratio Chapel. This retreat center has several chapels. I have much to be grateful for and blessings are abundant. As I finish my writing and prepare to leave the chapel, I approach the crucifix. I hold the feet of Jesus – kiss his feet – then comes tears. These are the tears of my spirit – "teach me, teach me." Is this consolation?

Oratio Chapel, Spirituality Center of Loyola

Monday, March 31, 2008

I am so happy I have Sister Lucy as my director. She is very perceptive and can see to my heart. I am praying today for the grace to just be with God and feel him loving me without needing to do anything.

At mass today, Sr. Noel gave a reflection about the Annunciation of Mary. Mary could not have said yes without know how much she was loved. Only when you know you are loved, can you trust and say yes.

Lord, please let me feel your love – because I want to say yes to you.

I hear him call me by name. Wow - no one has ever called me that! It must be him.

(JESUS)
Joanie, I love you.

Tuesday, April 1, 2008
Morning session with Sister Lucy. The grace I pray for today is to allow myself to be loved by Jesus and to trust that he loves me even with all my thinking that I am invisible to him. She also asked that I begin to pray with and continue to meditate on Mary's Yes-response.

Today I found the Chapel of Arantzazu.

Thank you Lord. Thank you My Lady. How sweet to find you both here.

Chapel of Arantzazu, Spirituality Center of Loyola

I love Father Mark's homily!! There is no such thing as generic grace. There isn't regular grace that everyone gets. No, there is only particular grace. God wants to give us the grace that fits our own individual need, our particular wound, our worry, our pain and our particular broken heart. He calls us by name in order to give it to use in particular. I think that's why I heard him call my name – he will give me my very own particular grace!!!

During the afternoon, I am praying with Jeremiah 31:1-14

Verse 3-4: 'I have drawn you to myself. You will be happy and dance merrily.'
I am dancing with my God. After hearing him call my name at mass today, I finally let the tears of joy flow. What grace, what grace!!!!

I'm back in the Oratio Chapel and I'm beginning my meditation on the Blessed Virgin and her response to God's call for her life. I want to have the same courage as her. So I'm going to think about her life.

Lord help me do this.

All at once, I have this image of Joseph and Mary riding on the donkey into Bethlehem. They arrive at the inn and Joseph goes inside to ask for a room. During my prayer, I speak to Mary in the voice of the Innkeeper's wife. It's my own voice and I'm fussing at the innkeeper for sending the couple to the stable.

<u>Wednesday, April 2, 2008</u>

Sister Lucy suggests that I ask for a deepening of the grace of yesterday – trust, love. She suggested that I stay with the scripture images I had yesterday about the Innkeeper's wife and her conversations with Mary and let it expand. She explained my experience to be imaginative contemplation which was taught by Ignatius. She also suggested that I write my own Magnificat. I am hesitate but will give it a try.

I am praying with scripture, Luke 1:39-45.

Mary, please help me to also say yes to your son. Guard my children, all 6 of them and Gabriel too. Protect and guard my dear Carl. Mary, how your heart must have broken to see what would come for your boy. I am sorry for all your pain.

Each time I enter into contemplation about Mary and her life, I hear the voice of the Innkeeper's wife speaking. She sounds just like me.

(GERTRUDE)

My Lady, your magnificat shows your wisdom — you know the heart of Our Lord so well. Sister Lucy suggested I write my own for all the Lord has done for me. I am not nearly as wise as you but my heart does have the desire to know the heart of God. He has done a lot for me and in me. My magnificat comes forth.

> *My soul dances with joy at the sound of the Father calling my name.*
> *I go to Him, unafraid and trusting, and rest myself. I am home at last.*
> *Thank you my Jesus, my Christ, for making*

the way that I might delight in my Father's company.

You, O Lord, are my salvation, my refuge, my sanctuary.
No enemy can reach me as long as I remain with you.
It is I you alone, my heavenly Father, that I place my trust and my hope.
It is you I love. You satisfy every desire of my heart.

I want to worship you all the days of my life.
Let me never be put to shame because my sin has come between us.
Show me your ways Father, show me your heart.
Let all that I am love you more each day.

I desire your will for me Father, your will.
All this I pray through your Son, Jesus Christ, my Lord and my Savior.
Amen.

Hey my Lady, I want to ask something of you. Would you please accompany me to your son? I believe that he calls me — but I am afraid of what he wants of me. You know those eyes of his – he seems to know what I've been up to – even before I've opened my mouth to tell. I don't want to put it off any longer. If you come with me – he won't be too hard on me – not that I don't deserve it.

I can be rough with that innkeeper husband of mine. Do you know, he wanted to give that stable again the other day? I said no way – nothing doing. Yes, I can be rough and I always want things done my way. I can be stubborn. I'm sure that doesn't surprise you, right? Do you think that's want he wants to talk to me about – my stubborn ways? I know I got it coming – I sin – no way around it.

You make me feel safe talking to you. Did I ever tell you how much I always wanted a friend like you? That husband of mine brought me to the inn when we were betrothed. That was about 30 years ago. The most friendship I've had was when a traveler came to the inn with his wife. It was usually only for a few days so we never had a chance to develop much of a friendship. It's hard to talk to someone who will listen and not judge. I came from the farmland just south of Bethlehem. I never got much education. What I know, I've learned from hard work, and honest living with my husband and our two children. He is a bit rough around the edges, but I dearly love him so. I love waiting on him.

Some days when I am doing the wash, I grab one of his shirts and give it a great big hug. I can love him even when he ain't in it.

And then there's my children — blessings to my soul they are!!!

You know my Lady, there are things of a woman's heart that are best shared with another of the same. You have been that same heart to me. I knew it the moment I saw you going into the stable. You have always listened to my going on and on about my family and all my foolishness. You never change my Lady. I thinks that's what I like best about you. You have remained my friend even when I knew you must get tired of hearing my stories. And you can cook — oh how I love your bread!! Something special happens when we have wine with it.

Thank you for coming with me today. What do you think your son wants? What does he want to tell me?

Back in my room for the evening. It has been exhausting — so much prayer — so many images — so intense — I've been writing non-stop all afternoon. I'm trying to write down every conversation between the Innkeeper's wife and Mary. If she talks with Jesus, I want to write it all down. I don't want to miss anything. This feels so real.

Thank your Lord for such big grace! I love you!

(<u>GERTRUDE</u>)

Oh my Lady, I am so glad I came to your son today. He is right – I gotta admit it. I'm a hard woman, stubborn, cold-hearted even, gotta have it my way. But my lady – it's the way he said it – the truth isn't always easy to hear and to see through his eyes – there are those eyes again. I told you about his eyes right? The day he was born, we both knew he had his father's eyes didn't we?

My Lady I'm so glad you never let go of my hand while I was with your son. It made me feel loved. It made it a lot easier to hear when your boy Jesus had to tell me. He told me something I never knew. He said I should go read it in the Psalms (51). I'm going to make my husband read it too. Jesus said I was a sinner, born a sinner. And if he said it – then it must be true. Then he tells me he loves me anyway.

He said I was born with the original sin of Adam and Eve. What a shame to have to carry their sin – but that is just what it is. C'est la veritie. But guess what? He also said how easy it is to be washed from that sin and all the others I have committed in my life. I think this is what you have been trying to get me to see all these years. I took a visit from you Son for me to finally get the whole picture.

My Lady, will you come with me every time I hear your boy call me for a visit? Thank you, I knew I could count on you to be with me. And you know what – from now on – you can count on me too!! You and Jesus both can count on me.

Thursday, April 3, 2008

Today I will pray with my magnificat. Today I will pray for the grace to have the same kind of passion as Ignatius for God. I go to the Chapel of Conversion in the upper level of the Basilica of Loyola and pray for intercession from St. Ignatius. I figure if I'm using his method of prayer, imaginative contemplation – he could help me with it.

Ignatius, you must have really felt like the prodigal son when you first felt the love God has for you. Your sin was grievous for you just as my sin is grievous for me. So this much, we have in common; you and I are sinners, and we have been welcomed back into the arms of the Father. So much love! So much love! It seems no matter how far away from him we stray, no matter the hugeness of our sin, his love is always ours for the accepting. You accepted it, and your passion for it never ceased afterward.

The grace I am praying for today is to know your kind of passionate love for the Father. St. Ignatius, it is here in this room that you asked our Lady to go with you to the Father. I have done the same here too. She and Jesus have agreed to walk with me to the Father. Come with us. Journey with me. Help me to prepare myself. I love the Father. I love his Son and my lady too.

But can I do this? Can I really go to the Father? I am in awe. I have no words to say to Him, yet I want to be with him."

Lord, I will try my best to avoid sin – and when I fail, I know that I am still loved – this you promised and I believe you.

Evening mass in the Chapel of Conversion. Father Mark's homily was about how good we feel when we are in close relationship with God. Then we get nervous and move away from him when we sin. When we look at our sin through our own eyes it doesn't look too bad. But, ask God to see what he sees when he looks at us.

Lord, please show me the woman you see when you look at me – sins and all. I want to see myself as I truly am.

Chapel of Conversion, where Ignatius
had an apparition of Our Lady.

Statue of Ignatius in the Chapel of Conversion.

Friday, April 4, 2008

Today, I am grateful that Mary and Jesus are revealing themselves to me in these contemplations. I pray for the grace to be present with the Father and not be afraid. I'm going to the chapel on the first floor. It's the main chapel for the retreat center and has a very large mosaic of the Jesus. I will go there to find and ask him and Mary to accompany me to the Father.

Main Chapel, Spirituality Center of Loyola

(GERTRUDE)

Thank you my Lady. Thank you Jesus for bringing me on this trip. Jesus, to think you really have time just for me – to make this trip with me – it's been a long journey for me you know – about 5000 miles from home.

I can see the Father right over there. He seems anxious to see me. I wonder why. What's he going to do? He seems so tall even though he is sitting. His robes are beautiful. I bet I could weave him a really pretty one.

But before we go over to him – tell me about him first. What do I say? How do I act? Do I curtsey, bow, bend my head, or kneel? I feel like crying all of a sudden. I mean wailing – like when mama died. Do ya'll remember that?

Help me Mary. Help me Lord. You have always been able to help me look honestly at things. That's why I love you so much. It's that "no kidding around" thing about you, and it's all in the eyes. So Lord, tell me about your father; I mean my father.

(JESUS)

Oh my darling daughter. How you make me smile. You light up my heart when I look into your eyes. Those green eyes are my favorite. I know you would be a special one when I placed you in your mother's womb. There may have been another there with you, but it was not to be a brother. That's a story for another time.

So you want to know about the Father? Yes, he is your Father. Daughter, he has been waiting for a long time for you to want to be with him. I've told him, 'she will come. She's stubborn, just like we made her, so it might take a while; and she has been hurt. Her pain runs deep.'

The Father is waiting. And I can tell you, it pained him to see your broken heart when Bradley betrayed you with his sin. You nearly strayed from your marriage vows. We know how hard the devil tried to convince you that you were entitled to go outside your marriage like he did and repay pain with pain. Many have prayed for you to be strong. So did your earthly mother. She knew your pain and your feelings of betrayal. She kept after me and the Father to keep you from this sin. She knew, and so did we, that you might never recover from the guilt that kind of sin would bring into your soul. Her intercession was mighty and we heard her. We delivered you from that temptation.

(GERTRUDE)

Oh Jesus, how can I thank you for saving me. You are so right – I was very close to that same sin. My conscience would have never let me rest for a moment if I had totally given in. The Father knows all about it, doesn't he?

(JESUS)

Well yes, daughter, where I am, so is the Father. That's why he is waiting. He has been watching for your arrival. He knows all about your temptation – those you overcame and those you didn't. He knows your heart my sweet little green-eyes soul, and so do I. We love what we see. Let's walk on – it's not much farther now.

(GERTRUDE)

But Jesus, if he knows all my stuff – I mean all my sins – how can I go to him. With you and Mary, it's different. You've always been with me. I can talk so easily to you. I mean, I held you in my arms when you were born in that stable a long time ago. I even changed your diaper as an infant. Oh Jesus, I know you are my Savoir – you saved my life. Your eyes tell me so every time I look at you. I know that you loved me from the beginning – you are in my heart.

But the Father, now that something is different entirely. He is so big; at least he seems so big. How can I approach? Mary – please take my hand – I'm scared. Both of you – each take my hand. My legs are wobbling. Could you maybe even hold me up? I'm not sure I can stand.

Oh Jesus, I feel you leading me. Thanks for not pulling. I can tell you are showing me the path to walk. Oh and here comes those tears again.

(MARY)

Don't be afraid my friend. This is the one place you should be the least afraid. The Father is not the Wizard of Oz like you used to think as a child. He is everything you have hoped and prayed that he would be. I promise. You know that our friendship over these years has always been based on honesty.

You needn't be afraid to approach the Father. Do you remember the name you heard Jesus call you? Joanie. Well he and the Father call you by the same name. They love you the same way. They call you by this particular name – there is no other they created like you Joanie.

They want you to come and be with them – nothing more. You don't have to do anything. You don't even have to make him a new robe. Just come – take my hand and the hand of my son. Let us take you to the Father.

(GERTRUDE)

Ok my Lady, I still don't know what to say or what to

do. Are you sure I couldn't make him a robe or something. It wouldn't take long – I could have it done in a day or two. We could come back then. Oh Ok – let's go.

(JESUS)

Dear Father, may I present to you this beloved daughter of ours. See her pretty green eyes willed with truth love and pure intention of heart. She is very nervous and has put this off for a long time. Father, bless her with a renewed spirit and a passion for telling others how much we love her and them.

She has finally overcome her fears and approaches. Shall we give her a new life? Shall we honor her intentions? They have been true, even when she has failed. Her sin is grievous, but the desire I find in her heart is to be with us. Accept her Father. She is a bit like Thomas. She doesn't doubt my sacrifice for her – she doubts our love for her. Let's show her how much we love her. She is like the lost sheep, finding her way back to us.

(GERTRUDE)

Oh my Father, I don't know what to say. Um....it will come to me in a minute. I have waited a long time to come see you. I always figured you were too busy. I'm nobody important. But now Father, I see that you really know me. You have known me all these years. Wow.

Father, may I come closer?

Father, you feel so good. Can you ever forgive me for putting this off? I'm sorry. Oh so sorry. I was scared. I mean really scared. You aren't so tall after all. Not like the idea I had in my head – he is too big and powerful to get close to. It is just not so.

Father, may I just sit and rest with you? May I just sit at your feet? I like feet. Did Jesus tell you? I like hands too. And eyes too. This feels all snuggly. Oh Father, I could have been here with you all this time. What shall we talk about? I have so much to tell you. You go first – I'll listen.

<u>(GOD, THE FATHER)</u>

It is so nice to have you hear next to me my daughter. I do so love those green eyes. You make me smile. I saw you from a distance, asking my son and his mother to help you get here. That is the right way to get here to me. I thought for a moment you might change your mind and put this off again. Your legs were wobbling pretty badly. I am happy you overcame your fears of me and came. You will never be sorry you did.

Yes, we have much to talk about. There is plenty of time. For now, let's just get used to being with each other. For now, make yourself comfortable my beloved daughter. Welcome home!

(GERTRUDE)

Oh Father, I love it here. May I stay forever? You have so much to teach me – I can feel it. You teach, Jesus teaches, Mary teachers and your Spirit teaches. There is so much to learn and I want to learn it all. I am anxious Father. But I do feel a calming of my spirit. I know that you are the one doing it. I thank you for such grace.

I walked outside this morning. The world you created is so beautiful. Thank you for giving it to me and all of us. Father, my journey to you has been long and hard. I have so much gratitude for your welcoming me near you. I never want to be far from you ever again.

There are so many people struggling with their own fears and obstacles that get in their way to coming to you. It must sadden you – this long wait. I see how you love us so. I'm sorry Father that it took me so long. I'm sorry. How can I help? How can I ease your sadness over those who don't know you like this? Now please, be gentle with me. I want to help, but I'm not the smartest or most eloquent. Let me help in some little way; you know, like St. Therese of Lisieux, from the sidelines. You know me and vainglory – it can get me in trouble sometimes. So Father, please let me help – and do no harm to anyone on their way to you.

Saturday, April 5, 2008

In my favorite chapel again, Oratio Chapel. Thank you Father for this day and for loving me. I thank you for a good night's rest. I went for a long walk this morning. Walked too far, now I have a big blister on my toe. I offer it up to you my Jesus.

You suffered so much more than this little thing for love of me.

(GERTRUDE)

Thank you Mary and Jesus for helping me to the Father. How sweet it is with him. You knew it would be. I had to find out for myself. I am grateful for your help and your guidance. Will you now teach me how to be with the Father? How to live with him dwelling within me?

I feel like my insides, the home where my heart and soul reside, aren't the same anymore. I have a new resident that has come to stay. I need to clean things up there. I know he is here and I never want him to leave – ever. How will I live now that he is here? Things just can't stay the same as they were before he arrived. I feel like I want to get rid of all the old furniture, old dishes, old clothes, old surroundings, and even old pictures. I want to get everything new — nothing is too good for Him. Now, I don't mean that I'm going home and throwing out all my belongings. I didn't really mean that exactly. Although I do have too much and could use some pairing down and simplicity

What I mean is that I need to take a long look at my insides. Will you help me to be a worthy dwelling place? I know he will expect things of me — to do the right things, to say the right things. How will I know? Help me to learn how to listen and hear him when he calls, when he guides. I believe I can already hear him. Mary, you heard him didn't you? When he sent the angel Gabriel to tell you about the birth of your son.

Did I tell you? I have a step-son named Gabriel. He died right after birth. Carl still grieves this loss. Carl's love is deep for the son that he never knew. Please comfort him. He misses his baby boy.

"Gabriel, please comfort your dad. Let him know that you are there, right there with the Father. He misses the earthly life you would have shared. Let him know that you have always guarded his steps and kept him from grievous sin. Tell him clearly, that you are safe, happy and in the choir of angels he hears when he prays. Thank you for your intercession on his behalf."

So my Lady, tell me about your life before the visit from Gabriel. I know that it surely changed everything for you.

(MARY)

Thank you Joanie for asking. I would love to tell you about my life. That's what friends do, right? Growing up, I always knew that something was different. When the other girls wanted to play, putting off their chores, it never bothered me to continue with mine.

I always loved to pray to the Father. Now that you know the Father, I shall call him our Father. OK? I especially loved when we had prayer all together as a family. It seemed these prayers were somehow stronger. I also loved to go off by myself and talk to our Father. I would tell him of all things I was willing to do for him — even die for him if he would ask it of me.

Our life was hard. There was a lot of work and little money, but we had each other and our family bonds were strong. My favorite times were sitting under the trees listening to the wind rustle the leaves. It's like God's voice whispering to me. You know what I mean — you've always liked that too. I didn't have to say anything — no words, no prayer — not even any thoughts. It was as though there was only our Father and me and that was enough.

So, on this particular day, when the angel came, I thought I might be dreaming. But my spirit told me it was no dream and I should open my heart to what he came to say. I knew the world would never understand how it was to be and I told him so. But, just like the whispering of the wind – I knew I was hearing from our Father. This was the moment I had been praying for – to do something, anything for Him.

So I said yes. I told Gabriel, "If it be your will, my soul magnifies the Lord to make him known to all so they might love and serve him too. I'm not sure what happened next, but somehow I knew. You know how you say sometimes, 'I know that I know that I know'. Well I knew that what this angel said to me was true. I was going to have a baby – a son and he was going to be Jesus. And Joanie, you know the rest of my story.

You asked me earlier in your prayer, how to know what it is our Father is asking of you. Just listen, listen and listen some more. There really isn't magical to it. Remember how you got it yesterday in the chapel when the Father greeted you. And don't forget to ask me and my son to help you. We will always lead you to the Father. You have a place with him that is all yours – your particular place.

So, trust your heart, trust your prayer – keep it pure – keep it honest and keep it big. That is your gift. Thank Him always for bringing you to himself, for his love, for his welcome, for his Son. Thank Jesus for what he did for you. He has kept you heart pure and has stood between you and sin more times than you are conscious of. Thank him for that. Always be grateful for what you have and be glad with that. Don't desire any more. Let our Father give you the abundance – it will be sweeter for you that way.

Do all these things daughter and you will be fine. Trust that he will show you all you need to know. Thank you for letting me talk to you today. You are a good listener. Did you know that about yourself? That's why your Directees love coming to you. They like your honesty. There are many more that will be coming. Just remember to let our Father do the talking – he knows what they need to hear.

Have I told you today that I love you? I love you. I am grateful you came to me in the stable that night when my son was born. You right, he does have his father's eyes. I'm glad you had the courage to take him in your arms. I've been waiting to give him to you so we can start our real, true companionship. Just like my son – you make me smile.

<u>10:00 pm, back in my room</u>
Hot shower will hopefully clear my sinus. No chapel visit tonight. I'll pray here. I walked all morning and now paying the price with my allergies. They are crazy bad.

Thank you Lord for Zyrtec. It was a great day with Mary — worth it all.

I am praying with a scripture Sister Lucy gave me this morning. Matthew 17: 1-13 describes the Transfiguration.

I don't understand it too well. I think you are trying to tell me Lord, that not everyone will understand my experiences during this retreat — all my conversations with Mary, with Jesus and especially with the Father. I should be careful not to throw my pearls to the pigs as you say.

I see another gift — the wisdom to ready Scripture and hear you speaking directly to me — to my particular needs and senses. I've read Scripture before and never heard your voice reading it to me — to my heart. Thank you Father for yet another extravagant gift. My soul magnifies your love for me. Show me how to grow in love for you.

Mark 10: 17-22 — The rich man.

Jesus, you told the rich man to sell all his possessions — did you mean it literally? I think you mean for me not to get so attached to anything or to money that it becomes an obsession and takes my focus off of you. I should be generous with everything I have. This I promise to do.

Sunday, April 6, 2008

The grace I pray for today is to remain with the Father. I think I'll go for a walk this morning. I see sheep up on the hillside out of my window.

Oh, Father, come, let's go see them.

I go out to that hillside – there's a gate. Do I dare go inside to get a closer look at those sheep? What if they chase me? I stand there for a while. If I leave the gate unlocked – I can get thru it easily if they chase me. I ease past the gate and walk slowly – the sheep are grazing at the hop of the hill. I'm walking on the path just below them.

Oh Father – then you give me such a wonderful insight.
The sheep are at peace with themselves and nothing can disturb that, not even an intruding curious human wanting a close-up. What grace? Lord, how extravagant you are to give me the same peace these sheep seem to have. Oh yes, Father, I know nothing can disturb the peace you have given me. I thank you for that with all my heart. I love you.

I hear the church bells ringing – must be nearly time for mass in the Basilica. If I hurry I can make it. The mass will be the Basque language, but I will be able to follow it. This is the treasure we have in our Catholic faith. Let's go!!

Sheep on hillside next to retreat center

<u>11:00 am Mass in the Basilica</u>
I'm so glad I brought my journal with me to mass.

Jesus, I told Sister Lucy this morning that the grace I was praying for was to be with you in a special way. She suggested I go to you in the Last Supper. It's got to be your doing – that I'm remembering that as I come in for mass.

(JESUS)

So my Joanie, you've been wondering about me and the Eucharist. Rest easy — stay in your pew — it's ok to stay even though you don't understand the language. I will take this opportunity to explain it all to you. Just watch and listen to me. It's perfect — you can see the mass being held and hear my voice.

You see, I came to save the world from its own self-destruction, from its own sinfulness. There are those who have lost their way. They don't even remember why they were created. I told the Father I would come so that they could remember and have the choice to love. I came because I love each one that we created — one at a time. I came to give hope and love and an eternal life to each and every one. And I did that. But once my sacrifice was done and that day had passed, I knew people would forget it. I also knew that I had to give you a way to remember it forever and ever, never to cease.

So, I gave you the Eucharist. Now I know you look at the bread and wine with your head. So, Joanie, I am asking you to please look at it through the same heart that allowed you to be brought to the Father. That is how you should look at the Eucharist. Yes, on human terms, it is bread and wine. On divine terms, my terms, it becomes my sacrifice again. Just for you. It becomes

*that which brings you salvation, hope and the ability
to love.*

*See, when the priest makes the sign of the cross over
the bread and wine – that is the moment you should be
looking at it with the eyes of your soul, eyes of your heart
– the eyes of the Father has given you. I have given you
the Eucharist to renew you – to refresh you.*

*If you ever feel like my voice that you are hearing so
clearly today becomes hard to hear – come back to me
in the Eucharist. My voice will become clear again and
you will renew your faith. The Eucharist will keep our
relationship strong and sustained. So come to me often.*

*Don't look for some big external miracle of the Eucharist
like some people do. You don't need it. Having me, the
Father and the Spirit inside you is miracle enough.
Your particular miracle is happing now and has been
happening since the first day you arrived here on
retreat. Your experience of hearing us and my mother
are all part of your very own miraculous grace. We love
you this much.*

*Thank you for staying for mass today so I could explain
myself to you. You've been needing to hear it. I know
that you have struggled with my real presence for a long*

time. You have been looking for my presence with you head, not your heart. I will help you to do this. All you need to do is stand faithful and keep receiving me.

10:00 pm – Chapel of Arantzazu

We are leaving for home tomorrow. I want to say goodbye to all the chapels in this retreat center. I have come to love each one. My experiences in each have been profound. I begin in the Chapel of Arantzazu. I have come to say adieu to this precious place, to pray my magnificat and to express my gratitude for the extraordinary gifts you and Jesus have given to me while in this chapel.

My Lady of Arantzazu, you came to be with me – allowed me to talk on and on – till I was ready to hear what you had to tell me. I came here for you Mary. You helped me to shift my focus to your son – my Lord and Savior. Thank you for leading me to him.

10:45 pm – Main Chapel

Thank you, thank you, thank you Father, my Lord and my God for leading me to your embrace here in this chapel. I was afraid to come here. I didn't like the BIG Jesus here. I know that it was my fear – my inability to be loved – to accept your love that kept me from coming to this chapel.

Thank you Jesus, my savior and Mary, my mother for being gentle with me as I walked this way to my Father. I am grateful, so grateful. Be my companions always. Never leave me please. I beg you. Never leave me. I pray my magnificat to you.

<u>11:30 pm – Chapel of Calvario (my hour of adoration each day was in this chapel)</u>
Thank you Lord for revealing yourself to me in the Eucharist and especially for explaining it to me. I get it. I look at the bread and wine with human eyes and I see just that. But when I choose to look at it with the eyes of my faith, my heart tells me that it is you, coming to make the way to the Father possible for me. For this extraordinary grace, I thank you. You love me and I love you back. I offer my magnificat prayer to you.

Chapel of Calvario, Spirituality Center of Loyola

12:00 am - Oratio Chapel
I've come to call this 'my chapel'.

Oh my sweet mother, Mary, Blessed Virgin, my Lady, my friend, my companion, how much do I love you. Oh so much!!

You have come to me and held my hand. You showed me how to open my heart to your son and let him in to love me. You allowed me to find my voice and speak to you, to your son and to my Father. You allowed me to go with you to the birth of your son, and to live with you during my prayer experiences. You shared the story of your incarnation which inspired my own incarnation so the Father could find me. You have been so tender with me, so patient. You are a wonderful teacher, the best companion and you will always be my friend, my mother, my Lady.

I am grateful for the images you have given me of you and your son. They touched my heart and enabled me to see my desire for the Father. I've always had it but didn't dare allow it to surface. I was too afraid. I didn't think I was worthy of notice. I realize now that I am still not worthy but I am noticed – and loved by you and your son and my Father.

Thank you for begin here with your son in this Oratio Chapel. Teach me how to sustain the fervor I feel in the days, weeks, years to come. I know that I'm going back to my life and it is good. I miss everyone. Come with me Mary. Let's love everyone together the way your son teaches. I will do as you have asked me. I will tell everyone I possibly can about our experience together these past days and what you and your son have taught me. What grace!! Big grace!!!

I am grateful to you and your son and I pray my magnificat to you. Come home with me.

Statue of Mary and Jesus in the Oratio
Chapel, Spirituality Center of Loyola